DARK DOORWAYS

DARK DOORWAYS

PEGGY CHRISTIE

ISBN-13: 978-0-9988878-7-6

Cover Illustration by Luke Spooner

Published by Dragon's Roost Press 2019

For Robert - thank you for always accepting,
and encouraging, my weirdness.

Why Be Normal? - *Reckless Abandon* anthology, Catalyst Press, 2002

Zombie Payback - *Appalling Limericks*, Sam's Dot Publishing, 2007

Til Death Do Us Part - *Necrotic Tissue* #12, Stygian Publications, October 2010

The Alley - *Black Ink Horror* Vol. II, Issue 4, Sideshow Press Publications, 2008

Surviving the Horde - *Vicious Verses and Reanimated Rhymes*, Coscom Entertainment, 2009

Raptcharrr! - *Not in the Brochure: Stories of a Disappointing Apocalypse*, 2011

Burnt Toast - *Erie Tales IV: Tales of the Apocalypse/Resurrection Mary*, GLAHW, 2011

Q - *The Siren's Call* e-zine, February 2003

Psychobabble - Kenneth Cain's Blog Contest, 2014

Homecoming - Inkitt Darkest Place in the World contest, (online), 2015

All other content original to this volume.

CONTENTS

KNOCKING ON DEATH'S DOOR

"If it has to do with Todd, then I don't care!"

My father and I watched as my mother continued stirring the soup in the saucepan, the telephone's incessant shrieking echoing through the small kitchen. The Caller ID displayed "Todd Grafton" in block letters.

"But it could be life or death," my father said, but mom just shook her head.

"What would that matter? He can't do anything anyway."

She had a point, so we simply stared at the phone until it finally stopped ringing. The answering machine never kicked on. My dad moved alongside my mom. He put his arm around her shoulders, thin and frail now from the cancer ravaging her body. She turned to smile at him. He tucked a loose flap of the headscarf above her ear, gently caressing her cheek.

The front door opened, then slammed. The windows shook with the sudden pressure change, and I turned to see Uncle Todd, my mother's twin brother, stomp into the dining area connected to the kitchen. He shook his cell phone in the air.

"I was calling you. Why didn't you pick up?"

My mother yelled at him over her shoulder. "Why should I? Has anything changed? Was he even home?"

Todd tucked his phone back in his pocket, and stared at the floor. When he didn't reply, my mother barked out a rough laugh, and kept cooking.

"I told you it was useless."

Todd pulled off his knit cap, then ran a hand over the short layer of peach fuzz across his head. Since he had gone into remission, his hair started growing back, and his energy and strength returned. I knew he felt guilty for getting better when my mother hadn't.

"But-" Todd began before she cut him off.

"But what, Todd? He didn't answer the phone. He didn't come to the door. He's obviously not home. Just drop it already."

"But his car was there, and I think I saw him in that big recliner with a beer."

My mother turned sharply, dropping the wooden spoon to the floor. The expression on her face was one I hadn't seen since I was a little girl, and she caught me playing with matches: utter disbelief. It was quickly followed by burning anger. While my dad bent to pick up the utensil, my mother strode over to Todd, and poked a finger in his chest.

"Are you telling me that son of a bitch is living it up while I'm over here dying?"

He flinched. From the poke or her glare, I couldn't say, but he nodded. My mother turned to my father.

"James, get my coat. We're going over there."

"Are you sure that's such a good–"

"GET MY COAT!"

My father ran past the rest of us to the front closet. She had such low energy these days, he knew not to allow this outburst to go to waste by arguing further. He held up her winter jacket as she jabbed her arms into the sleeves.

"Rita, you drive."

Keys already in hand, I led the procession – mom, dad, and a nervous Uncle Todd – through the back hall and into the garage. By the time we'd all piled into my ten-year-old Honda Civic, my mother's ire had deflated somewhat, but her eyes still shone with a bright fire. Cancer or no, she was going to give him a piece of her mind whether he wanted to hear it or not.

He didn't live more than a few blocks away, but it took over fifteen minutes to reach his house. The construction on Ferry Street rerouted us to Passage Avenue. There a busted hydrant flooded the roadway, so I turned on Toll Road, where a disabled mini-van blocked our progress.

By the time I got us to Sticks Crossing (no matter how many times he complained to the City Planning Board, the street name had never been changed to the correct spelling,) all of us were agitated and ready to pick a fight. Except for Uncle Todd, who looked like he accidentally ate a worm, and was imagining it crawling up his esophagus to freedom.

As I rolled my car to a stop in front of his house, my mother opened her door. My father scrambled out of the back seat and grabbed her arm, hoping to aid her progress.

She slapped at his hand. "I don't need your help."

My father stepped back, his eyes misting at the sting of her words. Her mouth loosened into a gentle smile as she placed a hand on his chest.

"I'll always need you, James, but this is something I have to do under my own power. While I still have some anyway."

He returned her smile. "Go get him, hon."

As my mother strode up the front walk, the three of us stood by the car. I leaned over to my dad.

"Do you think she can do it?"

"If anyone can talk this guy into action, it's your mother."

We shared a small laugh as I engaged the car alarm, then we followed my mom. When she knocked on the door, we stopped on the walkway, giving her some semblance of privacy.

No answer.

My mother knocked again, this time with a little more force. Still no one opened up.

She gripped the knocker. The ghastly contraption, not because of its cartoon skeleton face, but rather its rusty, ruined condition threatening tetanus to those not already dying, hung in the center of a pitted steel door. She slammed it repeatedly, the blows reverberating through the neighborhood. After another minute of silence, she leaned against the door, breathing heavy, and my dad ran to her side.

I leaned to my left to look through the front bay window. There he was, kicked back in his recliner chair and nursing a beer, oversized headphones strapped to his head over the hood of his black sweatshirt. If he could hear music through the thick fabric, certainly he could hear the damn door. Considering how everyone on the street was standing on their respective porches watching the now Grafton Family Spectacle, he had to be aware of our presence.

Maybe he was. Maybe he knew we were here, *why* we were here, and just didn't want to deal with it.

Well, too bad for him.

I turned to a well-manicured bush on my left, and squatted down. After digging through the dirt, I found a medium sized rock. I tossed it up and down, satisfied with its heft. As my father helped my mother stand on the porch, I walked up to the front window, and hurled the rock through it. The pane shattered and the rock sailed through the house, smacking him in the head, and knocking his headphones to the floor. He didn't move for a moment, simply sighed and looked down at the rock as it rolled to a stop. When he glanced up at me, I folded my arms in defiance, and jutted my chin at him.

He held up his hands in surrender, and pushed up from the chair. I turned to my folks. My dad stared at me, and my mother smiled.

"He's coming," I said, smug satisfaction puffing out my chest.

Within a few seconds, we heard the snap of a lock. Then another. A series of deadbolts, chains, tumblers, buttons, and levers clicked or screeched as he unlocked his door. When it opened, my mother straightened her back, and brushed my father's hands from her shoulders. It didn't do much to give her any kind semblance of authority as Death appeared in the doorway, his thin, ashen face and sunken eyes turned down toward her.

She cleared her throat. "Well, it's about time. Are you enjoying yourself in there?"

He shrugged, his mouth turned down in a sad, sagging expression. "I suppose I *was*, Kat."

My mother bristled, her lips pressed together into a straight thin line. She hated that nick name, but he continued to use it. At least he'd stopped calling her Puss.

"So I suppose you just love playing favorites, too?"

Death frowned. "What are you talking about?"

She pointed at Todd. When Death looked over at him, Todd held up his hands as if to say this wasn't his idea.

"You gave him a reprieve. He's my twin brother, so basically we're the same, but you saved him and not me."

"Well, *technically*, yes, you are very similar but–"

"Then why does he get to live while I have to keep dying like this?"

"Kat–"

"My name is Kathryn! Stop calling me Kat, and tell me why you're letting him live!"

Her voice squeaked at the peak of shrillness, and she slumped against my father. Death rubbed a knobby hand over his gaunt face, then sighed.

"Look, Kat...Kathryn. Exactly what do you want from me? You want the answers to death and dying? You want to know why we're all here, blah, blah, blah?"

She pushed away from my father, and edged closer to Death, her fingers folded together and clasped against her chest.

"Can't you do something? Anything?"

He stepped forward, and bent at the waist. His face, once hidden in the shadowed cowl of his hoodie, now hovered inches from hers. Frowning, his mouth twisted to the side, Death reached out a bony finger, and tapped my mother on her nose.

"*Boop.*"

She collapsed into a heap at his feet. The three of us stood motionless as we gawked at her crumpled body. I stared up at him as he waved a hand in our general direction.

"Now go away."

"What the hell?" I screeched, moving forward to demand some explanation.

Death growled, a low rumble like rolling thunder. He began to stretch upward, his frame doubling, then tripling in size. I stepped back as his black sweats morphed into a thick velvet robe that flowed with serpentine grace. What little flesh covered him fell away in ribbons to reveal a stark white skeleton, each bone clacking into place with a heavy thud as he grew.

I quickly realized why his house didn't have a decorative roof over the porch. By the time he'd taken his regular form, his eight-foot frame towered over us, and we cowered in his shadow. His voice shook the windows of half the houses on the block.

"You *dare* to question me?"

"No, no she doesn't, your honor."

My father pulled me back, then motioned for Todd to come closer. He shook his head, and took a few stumbling steps away. Grumbling, my father pulled on my jacket.

"Help me take her home."

He had already bent to place his hands under my mother's arms, jerking his head toward her feet. I shuffled over, and grabbed her ankles. On the count of three, we lifted her up, and slowly maneuvered her down the small set of steps. I turned to look at Death. He'd already begun to shrink down to his more human façade. He gave me one final glare as he mumbled.

"Now I'll have to report this to the authorities. My ass will be in a sling for taking her ahead of schedule."

I nearly dropped her as I stared at him. He arched a pasty eyebrow.

"What, you thought I was neglecting my duties? Maybe taking a vacation or something? You people."

He shook his head in disgust, then looked at me, pity

creasing his brow. "I don't decide who lives and who dies, Rita. I just work here."

He turned on his heel and slammed the door, leaving me to stare at empty space as I clutched my dead mother's ankles.

SURVIVING THE HORDE

Whispers, quickly turning to sighs.
Low moans carry forward to my ears.
The wind blows my way and I
Smell them.
Rot. Decay. Death.
Gone, but they return.
Broken, but they move.
Dead, but they feed.
We are small in number now,
Hunted, prey. The living.
Scrabbling our survival in the dirt,
In the dark.
They have taken our place and we theirs.
When, why, and how are no longer important.
Dominance belongs to them even if they are unaware
Of their power.
Move, protect, hide, live. All that matters.
My scent on the wind and they redirect.
I can run, but not forever.

They have forever. They have all the time
In the world.

ZOMBIE PAYBACK

A man hung himself with a hose.
His wife used voodoo, so he rose.
Now back from the dead
He stroked her sweet head
And sucked out her brains through her nose.

THE ALLEY

She stared into the empty alley. The afternoon sun blazed overhead, burning her exposed skin, and the quiet breeze dried the sweat as it trickled down her back. She scratched absently as it tickled its way down her skin, and under the waistband of her slacks. Although she stood two feet in front of the opening to the alley, it was draped in darkness. She couldn't see beyond the facades of the buildings that cradled the gloom. She reached out her hand, and watched as it disappeared into the blackness. Pulling it back quickly, sucking in her breath, she almost believed her hand had separated from her wrist, and she'd look down to see a ragged stump pumping blood out onto the sidewalk, each drop sizzling as it splashed onto the burning concrete.

Staring back into the empty blackness, she began to sway back and forth. She felt her arms go slack at her sides. Her breathing slowed and deepened as if on the verge of sleep. She took a tentative step towards the alley, then another. Her head fell back, a smile curling her lips. She raised her arms, wiggling her fingers as if testing the wind.

She then clasped her hands together as if embracing a lover. She didn't so much step as glide into the darkness of the alley. Her scream of horror and ecstasy were swallowed by the dark void as she disappeared from the light.

Pauline blinked. She looked again out her fifth-floor office window, rubbing her eyes to clear them. She must have been seeing things. One minute, a young woman was standing at the opening to the alley across the street, and the next minute she was gone. She first noticed the woman when she stuck her hand into the shadows and pulled it back, almost afraid, as if she thought it had been chopped off or something. When she started swaying back and forth, and then raised her arms, Pauline was truly intrigued. She figured the woman was tripping out on the latest trendy drug, and was having her own private little party right there on the sidewalk of downtown Detroit.

Not that that would be completely unusual, but she didn't look like the typical druggie. She had on a crisp, white, short-sleeved blouse, well-pressed, black, cotton pants, and black pumps. Her hair was pulled up in a French twist, and Pauline could see her gold wristwatch twinkling in the sunlight when she raised her arms. She had started chuckling to herself just as the woman threw back her head, screamed, then disappeared. Pauline shook her head, stunned. She tapped the Computer Services tech on the shoulder.

"Hey, Mike. Did you see that?"

Mike, who was working on her computer since it crashed forty-five minutes ago, grunted. "See what?"

"That woman. She was standing in front of that alley, and now she's gone."

"Pauline, I've had my face in your hard drive for the past half hour. The only things I'm seeing are chips, wires, and circuits, okay?"

"What? Oh, yeah. Right. Sorry. Um, I'll be right back."

Pauline grabbed her suit jacket, and headed for the elevators. Once on the ground floor, she raced through the lobby to get outside. Discarded scraps of dirty paper, dead leaves, and grit were caught in the wind tunnel between her office building and the parking garage next door, and danced around her. The City County building hulked like an ogre to her right, and she could just make out the shining towers of the Renaissance Center over the roof of the parking structure.

As she slipped on her jacket, a particularly ornery receipt from Foran's Irish pub down the street smacked her in the eye, causing it to water. She ripped it away, and continued toward the alley, wiping at her tears with the sleeve of her jacket.

She stared across the street at the opening to the alley, and her steps faltered. By the time she reached the curb, Pauline was trembling. She felt a shiver slink down her spine and slip into her shoes, turning her feet to ice. She shook with fear, and she had no idea why. The blackness of the alley before her was like any other set between the towering office buildings downtown. Solid, thick, and holding things inside it that you could only see once you braved the entryway. But Pauline didn't want to know what lay hidden in its depths.

She crossed the street anyway, pulled against her will. Her navy pumps scraped along the sidewalk as she tried to drag her heels and prevent her forward progress. It was of no use. Pauline continued walking toward the darkness. She looked around frantically for anything to grab onto, but the pulling sensation finally stopped. She stood a few feet away from the alley breathing heavily, fearing that her pounding heart would burst right through her chest.

She looked at the sidewalk and saw a bright flash. She reached down, and picked up a gold wristwatch. It must have belonged to the young woman who was standing there a few minutes before. She remembered seeing it on the woman's wrist as it reflected the bright sun, but Pauline had begun to believe that she had imagined the whole spectacle. So, she was relieved, and terrified, as she turned the watch over and over in her hands.

Pauline looked up at the entry to the alley. She squinted her eyes thinking it would help to penetrate the thick shadows. Just then a man stepped out of the blackness, scaring the be-jesus out of her. She jumped, dropped the watch, and a small scream escaped her lips.

"Oh, I'm so sorry. I didn't mean to scare you. The way you were looking in there I thought you could see me."

Catching her breath Pauline waved it off. "Oh, don't worry about it. I was trying to see into the alley but it's just too dark. I was looking for the woman who was wearing that watch. She was standing here a few minutes ago but just disappeared. I thought maybe she went in there."

The man smiled and shook his head. "I didn't see anything but rats myself. I dropped my money clip, and it bounced into the alley. Luckily I can see pretty well in the dark, but I didn't see any woman. Sorry. Was she your friend?"

"Uh, no. I didn't know who she was. I just... well, I heard her scream, and I wondered what happened to her, that's all."

"Just concerned for your fellow man, eh? Don't see much of that around here these days."

She flushed and held out her hand. "Well, I don't know about that. Uh, I'm Pauline, by the way. Pauline Garrison."

"Oh, where are my manners? I'm sorry. I'm Marcus Connelly. I really am sorry I frightened you."

"That's all right. No harm done, right?"

He smiled, and Pauline really looked at him for the first time. He stood about six feet tall, slim and athletic, with broad shoulders and a thin waist. His hair was short and streaked with silver, so she put him at about forty years old. He had a few smile lines around hazel eyes that twinkled over a thin nose and full lips. He had a few days stubble on a square jaw, and was dressed as if he'd just returned from a hunting trip. It was almost eerie how he looked exactly like her idea of the perfect man.

"You look like you just got back from a trip Up North. Are you a hunter?"

Marcus looked down at his navy-blue suit and tie, and frowned at Pauline in confusion. "Excuse me?"

"You know, with the flannel and–"

Pauline faltered. When she first saw him, he was wearing a navy and white flannel shirt with black jeans, and dark brown hiking boots. Now as she looked at him, he was dressed more like an Advertising Executive at her firm than a hunter. She shook her head.

"I... I'm sorry. I could have sworn you were wearing flannel a minute ago."

He chuckled. "My suit's not that bad, is it?"

When she looked down at her shoes in embarrassment, he quickly apologized. "Don't worry about it. Your eyes probably hadn't adjusted from looking in the darkness of the alley, that's all."

She nodded, chewing on her thumbnail and feeling like a complete idiot. "Well, it was nice to meet and insult you, Marcus Connelly. I guess I'd better get back to work."

"Well, wait. Are you doing anything for lunch?"

The alley now forgotten, she put her hands on her hips. "Do you always invite women who make complete fools of themselves out to lunch?"

He smiled down at her, his hazel eyes shining with an almost ravenous intensity. "Always."

It was his voice, maybe, or the way he was looking at her, she didn't know. But when he stepped closer to her, forcing her head to tilt back to look at him, an overwhelming desire to kiss him surged through her. Her stomach flopped with something akin to butterflies, but stronger. More like turkey vultures. She slid her hands up the front of his suit jacket, and locked them behind his head. He laced his fingers in her hair, pulling her mouth to his. When they kissed, fire seared through her mouth, down her throat, across her stomach, and took up residence in her groin. Clamped together in an unbreakable vise of lust, which she neither wanted nor tried to release, he slowly inched their bodies toward the opening to the alley. Before they crossed the threshold, he broke free and took one step into the shadows.

Only his head, left shoulder, and leg were in the sunlight, his left hand reaching toward Pauline, beckoning. His eyes clouded, and became as black as a vast ocean in the night. She took a tentative step toward him, wanting more than anything to have his lips on her again. He took another step back, his face and hand the only things protruding from the dark. He waved her forward and spoke. His voice was as smooth and thick as an oil slick.

"Come, Pauline. It's time to eat."

She smiled and laughed, her ecstasy heating her face.

She reached for his hand, grabbing it as if her life depended on it. As he guided her into the alley, his eyes suddenly flared with silver flames, and he crushed her hand in his now slime coated grip. Pauline screamed, then disappeared into the black.

Mike smacked the worthless computer on Pauline's desk in disgust. He'd been hunched over the damn thing for nearly an hour, and his back spasmed in protest. He stood, stretching his cramped muscles, and looked out the window. He saw Pauline standing across the street in front of an alley. He frowned as he watched her. She just stood there, her arms slack at her sides with her head tilted back. If he didn't know any better, he would have thought she was high on something. He shrugged, and turned back to the computer, growling as he looked at the open panel and all its exposed wires and circuits. He bent over it again, hoping he could get it fixed by the time she got back.

Several minutes later, a young man in a grey business suit, ran through the courtyard, his coattails flapping behind him. He hesitantly crossed the street, and stopped in front of the alley, staring into its dark opening. Shaking in fear, he wondered what had happened to the young brunette who was standing here just a minute ago.

LONG PIG

The offal exploded in a smear of viscous gore against the window. A light clicked on inside the house. Children's laughter floated on the evening breeze as the patter of running feet echoed in the dark. The front door opened, and the man shouted at the retreating Devil's Night pranksters.

"I'm calling your parents!"

"No, you aren't."

"But honey–"

"I told you not to hand out the gristly scraps after last year's Halloween BBQ. These kids want fresh meat."

She looked back at the portly man, hog-tied and whimpering, in the corner.

"Trust me. They won't target us next year."

INVADERS

The rest of the team lay on the floor. The lucky ones had already died. The unlucky were immobilized in sticky pools of black goo, strings of bloody slime stretched across their arms and legs. I watched as Christian's skin split along his naked torso, and a wave of dark red spheres spilled out. Each orb doubled, then quadrupled, continuing to multiply exponentially. The replicating conglomerate floated to the center of the laboratory, directly in front of the growing tear in the space-time continuum. A crimson army lay in wait on the other side. Dear God, what have we done?

'TIL DEATH DO US PART

"Hey, Steve?"

"Yeah, Mike?"

"How long do you suppose we've been sitting here?"

Steve looked around the brightly lit kitchen, glancing over the cherry wood table between him and his best friend. The combined stench of both their rotting bodies would have choked a normal human being into convulsions by now. Unfortunately, neither he nor Mike was a normal human being anymore. No one was. He shrugged his shoulders.

"I don't know. A week or two maybe. Why?"

"No reason. Just wondering."

Steve nodded, and looked out the sliding glass door to his left. Mike's backyard stretched out over an acre of grass and weeds, ending in a dull green expanse of pine, maple, oak, and birch trees. A haze, the color of two-day old vomit, hovered just above the line of the forest like dirty gauze. As Steve wondered when he'd last seen any animals, or anything alive, roaming near those woods, Mike cursed.

"Shit."

"What's wrong?"

"Look."

Mike held up his left thumb. The ragged end that used to be attached to his hand dripped black viscous fluid onto the table. He wiggled his remaining fingers as if to test the strength of their connections, then pushed his detached thumb against the oozing stump as if trying to will it back onto his hand. But it fell to the table, bounced twice, and rolled to a stop.

Steve pointed to the nail clippers in Mike's right hand. "You were cleaning your nails again, weren't you?"

"Well, yeah. But I didn't think–"

"Exactly. Didn't I say you shouldn't do that? Mike, we've been rotting here for about a month now. You've got to stop picking at yourself before you come apart completely, got it?"

Mike nodded, his lips pursed in a pout, and turned the shiny silver nail clippers in his hands.

"Stupid," he said as he pulled back his arm and threw the clippers into the corner. Steve heard a wet, tearing sound, and watched Mike's expression go from panic to anger as he reached his hand under his shirt, and rubbed it over his skin. He rolled up the short sleeve, and black ooze seeped out from his shoulder.

"Dammit! I think I ripped my shoulder."

Steve shook his head and sighed. "Mike, look at me."

Mike turned to look at his friend, rolling his sleeve back into place.

"Do you see any of my fingers falling off? Is my skin ripping open at various places? Do I or do I not still have all my extremities intact?"

"Well, your nose is a bit on the black side, and your skin looks like the color of Jim's old Chevy. You know, the one we used to call 'The Gangrene Machine.' Do you remember when he used to–"

"Mike, that's not the point!"

Mike looked down at the table. Steve reached over and patted his arm.

"I'm sorry. I didn't mean to yell at you. The point I'm trying to make is that I'm not doing anything that will speed up my deterioration. Yes, I'm dead and rotting away, but if I start slamming my hand down, or throwing things around, I'll fall apart faster than I already am. Do you understand?"

Mike nodded. "But, Steve, don't you want this to end sooner rather than later?"

"No. I'm not ready for that yet. I guess I haven't reached the point where I'd rather be truly dead than live like this. But I've always–"

Steve felt his nose split and slide off his face. It plopped onto the table in front of him with a wet smack. He picked it up, and cradled it in his palm. The cells broke down so rapidly that what he used to consider his best feature turned into a small puddle of chunky, black slime in his hand while he watched. He looked up at Mike who tried to cover a smile, and failed.

When Mike began to snicker, Steve ground his teeth in anger, reaching his arm back to throw what was left of his nose at Mike's face. He skipped that plan when four of his teeth popped loose. He spit them out into the same hand holding the remnants of his nose. Mike stopped laughing, reached over, and plucked one of the loose teeth out of Steve's hand. He held it up to the light as if inspecting a newly cut diamond.

Placing it back in Steve's palm, Mike grinned. "Are you sure you're not ready yet?"

Steve grunted in response, and carefully lay the remaining chunks of flesh on the table, lining up the four loose teeth beneath them. He studied the partial face he had created and sighed. Mike kept smiling, and after a few minutes, Steve joined him. His grin turned to a chuckle, and soon they were both laughing. How could they do anything else?

The entire situation was absurd. The deadly haze had crept into the town, slithering into and over everything and everyone as it passed. It took up residence just over the trees a week later, and hadn't moved since. No one knew what caused it, who started it, or why. Did it really matter now anyway? Shortly after its arrival, everyone started to die.

Cats and dogs were the first to perish. Most of them keeled over and lay still, no matter if they were the greatest of Danes or the tiniest of Chihuahuas. When their owners wrapped them up in old blankets for burial or to take to the vet, the animals would shake, cough, then get up as if nothing had happened. It wasn't until a few days later that people would realize their pets were dead. It was hard to ignore the smell of the animals' rotting flesh, or the sight of it falling off in furry chunks after Fido had a flea-scratching frenzy.

Soon after, birds plummeted out of the sky, squirrels and raccoons collapsed on the side of the road, and even the flies dropped like, well, flies on windowsills or mid-air. But within minutes, they all recovered and went about their normal daily routines, albeit just a little deader for the wear.

At first it seemed only the animals were affected. Maybe the people got lucky, and the brown haze hadn't been designed to wipe out human life. When Sally Brandt started mowing her lawn in her neon pink bikini, and her breasts fell off right after she maneuvered around the huge maple tree in her front yard, Steve knew they were all doomed.

Steve grimaced as he remembered the last time he drove his truck. He was headed home from the store. His skin had been itching all day, and he had gone out to get some more calamine lotion. He'd spotted the last bottle behind two women who were arguing over it like it was the last pork chop in a world gone vegetarian. As the one ripped off the other's arm and proceeded to beat her with it, Steve plucked the lone bottle off the shelf, and scurried out of the store.

On his way home, his legs had tingled and spasmed. Twice his right leg cramped and his knee locked in place, forcing his foot down on the accelerator, making it impossible to move. The truck raced at fifty miles an hour down Main Street. He'd almost run over Mrs. Carmichael and her Schnauzer, Bootsy.

When his leg finally relaxed, and he could reduce the truck's speed, Steve realized he was still a long way from home, but only minutes from Mike. He headed there instead. He didn't want to be on a busy street if his leg locked up again. Plus, he didn't want to go home where he would be alone. As he'd turned onto Mike's driveway, his arms cramped and his leg spasmed again. The truck bounced over the driveway and onto Mike's front lawn, crashing to a halt against the evergreen outside the front door.

Mike had helped Steve inside, and sat him down on the living room sofa while the cramps subsided. He didn't want to risk driving again, so he stayed with Mike from that day on. After another week of painful cramping, Steve sat at the kitchen table and hadn't moved since.

He and Mike laughed for another ten minutes over that memory. Steve jerked his thumb towards the front door.

"I'm really sorry about that, man."

Mike waved his hand in dismissal, and wiped at the tears that *would* have been streaming down his face had his tear ducts still functioned. Grinning, he pointed at Steve.

"You know what's really funny about that? The fact that yuuaawhh...."

In mid sentence, Mike's jaw dropped to the table. He raised his eyebrows, rounding his eyes as he stared at Steve, as if he didn't want to look down and see the detached part of his face laying in front on him. Steve felt his own eyes widen, and wondered if they reflected the anguish in Mike's.

Finally, Steve looked away, and stared out at the yard. He could hear Mike as he picked up his jaw, then rotate it in his hands. When Steve turned to watch him, Mike placed his mandible gently on the table, then met Steve's gaze. His blackened tongue wiggled like a fat, bloated slug as he tried to speak.

"When doo you hink we'll rehlly die, Shtee?"

Steve stared down at his rotted nose and Mike's jaw. He gazed out the glass door again, watching the haze as it hung over the trees. Sighing, Steve looked back at his friend, and studied the ruin his face had become. He pushed up from the table to move closer to Mike, hoping to comfort him.

A great, sloppy rip echoed through the kitchen. Steve looked down to see his bottom half still in the chair, and his upper body, dangling entrails and all, swaying on the support of his rotting arms. He had been sitting in this chair for over a week. Most of his bodily fluids had pooled into his backside, making his lower half much heavier than the upper.

He lowered his torso back onto his hips, then tucked the stray loops of intestines back inside his abdomen. Wiping the sticky residue onto his shirt, he stared into Mike's wide eyes. Steve's voice shook from fear, and rot.

"Soon, I hope."

THE EYES HAVE IT

Wide, frightened eyes stared back at him from beneath the clear, thick plastic. Though he had killed her over an hour ago, she kept staring at him. Watching him. Accusing him.

"What the fuck are you looking at, huh?"

She didn't answer. Just stared.

"I didn't make you look like her, did I? I didn't ask you to dress like her, or smell like her. It's not my fault."

The eyes – so clear, so blue. Staring.

"If...if anything, it's *your* fault."

"I know, Linus."

Her lips didn't move, but he heard her, clear as day. Even in death, he could hear her. She always knew how to get into his head. Ever since he was a boy, she'd had immense power and control over him. He hated it.

"That's right," he said.

"I know, Linus, that you're weak. Just like your father. Weak, and a coward, and useless. You know what I mean by useless, don't you, Linus?"

"Stop it."

"Useless between your legs. You should have been born a girl for all the worth you've got in that soggy noodle you call a penis."

Linus clamped his hands over his ears. "Stop it."

"You never were able to satisfy me, son. And if you couldn't make your mother happy, how can you ever expect to please another woman?"

He shook his head back and forth as her tirade continued.

"Like that waitress in Omaha? Or the real estate agent in Minneapolis. Even the hotel maid in Detroit. You couldn't get it up for any of them, could you, Linus? Just like you couldn't for me."

"Shut up! Shut up!"

"You never loved me, even after everything I did for you. I slaved at two jobs to make sure you had food on the table, and clothes on your back. I raised you all alone. No man around to help me. Hell, didn't need one. Didn't need some drunken welfare case to raise you to be a man. And what thanks did I get? None. What did I get in return for all my sacrifices? A limp-dick, coward of a son, that's what."

Linus slammed his fists against his temples. He couldn't let her get away with it. Not this time. He looked around the cellar, his gaze falling on a pile of round weights sitting in the far corner. He ran to them, and picked up a twenty-pound disc.

Gripping it tightly, he strode back over to her. He could feel the tears dampen his cheeks, then cool his skin as they dried. Linus lifted the weight above his head, and screamed.

"I loved you!"

The eyes beneath the plastic, those cornflower blue

eyes, stared at him until he brought down the weight, again and again, and crushed their accusations into a gooey mass of blood and tissue.

Blessed silence. Finally, he was free of her. In his heart, though, he knew it was temporary. She always came back to him. It didn't matter if he changed his name or moved away, she would find him. But this time would be different. He could feel it.

After dumping her body in a lake two towns over, Linus found himself driving through the quaint downtown of a near-by city. Boutiques, stationery stores, "shoppes" selling various knick-knacks or trendy clothing, dotted the main drag. A dark, red Chevy exited a parking spot ahead on his right. He decided to pull his car into the vacancy, then walk around and explore.

Most of the stores didn't pique his interest until he came upon a small, independent bookstore called "Words and Things." He pushed open the door, and a bell chimed over his head. A voice from somewhere at the back of the shop called out.

"Make yourself at home and look around. If you need any help, just holler!"

"Um, okay. Thanks," Linus replied.

Shaky towers of tomes dotted various crossroads of aisles. Floor to ceiling shelves were crammed to bursting with books. He ran his fingers along each one, puzzling out the unorganized filing system by author, or title, or perhaps both.

As he rounded a corner, he collided with someone carrying a cumbersome stack of old encyclopedias. They toppled to the floor in a giant, musty heap.

"Oh, God. I'm so sorry," Linus said.

The woman, her dark hair twisted into a bun at the nape of her neck, bent down to pick up the fallen books. "No, no, it's my fault. I was carrying too many, and couldn't see where I was going."

"Let me help you."

Linus bent down to pick up one of the thick heavy books when she looked up at him.

"Thank you so much. Again, I'm really sorry."

Her eyes, her cornflower blue eyes, stared at him from behind black, wire-framed glasses. He felt the familiar heat build between his legs, but when she blinked, the warmth faded, along with any inklings of an erection.

It didn't matter. He'd just met her. Maybe after he got to know her better, things would be different. He moved too fast with the others. That's why he couldn't perform. He didn't know them. He didn't know them at all.

"What about your mother?"

Linus frowned at the woman. "What did you say?"

"I asked if you could get that other one, by your foot."

He looked down at the book on the floor. "Oh, yeah. Sure."

Linus picked it up, and followed the woman to a cluttered desk at the back of the store.

"Maybe just put them over here."

She set her books down on the floor next to the desk, and Linus did the same. When they straightened, they clunked heads.

"Ouch! I'm so sorry. Again," she said, laughing.

Linus rubbed his forehead and smiled. "No worries. I've got a thick skull."

"Well, thank God for that."

"What's your name?"

"I'm Angie. I own this place. And you are, besides the latest victim of my clumsiness?"

"I'm Nick. Nice to meet you."

He held out his hand, and she took it, offering him a strong grip and another warm smile. Yes, things would be different this time.

FILTHY

The mud-filled pit bubbled and churned at her feet. Flames from the surrounding torches licked the cave walls, their smoke tendrils coating the low ceiling with soot. Names, dates, and spells from eons of magical practitioners covered every exposed inch of rock.

She stood over the hole, waving her hands through its rising heat. "Come forth, I command thee. Bring your knowledge and power to me. As it harm none, so mote it be."

The sludge roiled and bulged, as if something began to form in its depths. A large mud sphere rose before her. She smiled, and reached out a finger to break the bubble's skin.

When it popped, a tiny yellow, fuzzy chick floated in the air.

"Peep."

She dropped her arms to her sides, and stomped her foot in frustration. "Oh, COME ON!"

The fluffy bird blinked twice at her.

"Peep."

GRACEFUL

She tiptoed across the linoleum floor, slick with blood from three people hanging upside-down from the ceiling. She'd slit their throats to begin the draining process, but forgot to place the collection buckets beneath each one. A few pints had splashed everywhere before she rectified it.

Now, she flitted and danced around the puddles, trying to avoid the mess. She needed to clean all this up by the time Don returned. Before she reached the utility closet, he threw open the door, startling her. She jerked in surprise, and her feet flew out from under her.

Landing in the middle of a blood puddle, red fluid splattered all around. She landed with a heavy thud, and pain shot up from her tailbone to the top of her skull. As she rubbed her aching head, smearing blood through her blonde hair, Don laughed.

"Smooth move, Ex-Lax."

FAT

Each person carried the weight of three average individuals. That didn't stop them from gathering each month at their favorite restaurant to savor full meals, sometimes two or three, from the "Secret Menu." Which wasn't that big of a secret, by the way, but they liked to pretend they were special and exclusive.

Using home-brought utensils and napkins – because no one wants to be a *basic* glutton – they dipped into the smorgasbord before them, and shoveled forkfuls of food into their gaping maws. The slurps of spittle on greasy lips melded with the sloppy, wet chewing of stale bread, wilted vegetables dripping in oils, bloody remnants of steaks, and partially molded fruits.

For several minutes, no one spoke, only savored the heady aromas from the dumpster they had surrounded.

At one point, Roger reached across Daryl to grab a half-eaten custard tart. Like a shark in a blood frenzy, Daryl grabbed Roger's meaty hand, and shoved it into his mouth, chomping down, and severing the top third from Roger's pinky.

"Dammit, Daryl. That's the second knuckle I've lost this year. You and Stan need to pay closer attention."

Carl pointed his fork at an empty space opposite him at the trash bin.

"Where is Stan anyway?" he mumbled around a mouthful of day-old, possibly two, spaghetti.

Margaret, the lightest at 265 pounds, answered as tomato sauce and masticated clams dribbled down her chin.

"He called me yesterday. Something about a heart attack. I don't know. The call got cut off."

"Oh, okay."

The silence returned as the group continued eating.

CUTHBERT, MI

Mary Ellen stood before the broken and faded sign at the city limits: *CUTHBERT, MI. FOUNDED 1814. POP: 274.* She flipped through a small notepad, double checking her research.

"Yep, this is it."

She smiled at James, who stood next to her, his face crinkled with doubt and worry. He studied the dirt road before them. Pocked with ruts and deep holes, his eye traveled along it, then fell on Copper Mountain looming in the distance.

"Are you sure about this, Mar? I mean, I know you think this is necessary to make your thesis complete but..."

He trailed off and held out his arm toward the road, and the small town that lay at its end. "You're gonna be out in the middle of nowhere. I mean, *No. Where.* I'm worried."

She rolled her eyes, and headed back to the car. She didn't want to have this discussion again. "James, I'm not a novice camper. I've been tent camping my whole life. I'm only gonna be here a couple days. What could go wrong?"

He opened his mouth but she held up her hands.

"I have a SAT phone, emergency medical kit, inclement weather supplies, and enough food and water for at least three days. I chose to do this in the summer for my best chance at good weather. Professor Hartman signed off on it last semester because he thought it was a great idea."

"But – "

"The socio-economic impact of the booming lumber and copper mining industries on this town, and why it was abandoned after only two years, has never been explored. Also, no other industries have ever succeeded for more than six months until, eventually, the entire area was abandoned."

"I know but – "

"I could end up being the first person to find out what really happened out here and why. Don't you want me to be the one to discover the truth?"

"Of course, I do."

"You do think I'm capable of handling myself, right?"

"Absolutely."

She batted her eyes are him and pressed each index finger into the dimples on either cheek. "Even though I'm just a little ol' girl?"

He tried to hide his smile as it stretched wide, but ended up laughing, and pulling her into his arms.

"I know you always do great at whatever you put your mind to. *That* doesn't worry me. It's everything else."

She leaned back and looked up at him. "What do you mean?"

"You know what I'm talking about."

She swatted his arm, then opened the trunk of their SUV. "Ppphhhhttt. That's all hearsay and gossip. Local superstition, nothing more."

"Maybe," he said, "but you have to admit, all that stuff is pretty damned unsettling."

She snorted as she heaved a large pack onto her back. Shaking open a map of the area, she grinned. "Then I guess it's good that I have my crystals and tarot cards with me."

He arched an eyebrow at her and she held up her hands. "Sorry, no offense intended to GiGi, okay?"

"She doesn't think you being here is a good idea either, you know."

"Ooooooo," Mary Ellen said as she waggled her hands in the air.

She could feel his disapproving gaze on the back of her neck as she studied the map, and walked toward the city sign. His grandma could believe all that hoodoo crap she wanted. It wasn't going to change her plans one bit.

Tracing her finger along the lined paper, Mary Ellen plotted her approach to the abandoned town. It would be easy to get there. One road in and out that was maybe two miles long. The mines were a couple miles beyond the center of town, but she might not need to go that far. The hard part would be finding a suitable campsite.

James' hands were suddenly on her shoulders and he spun her around to face him. She didn't want to fight, but readied herself for another argument. Instead he pulled her close and kissed her, a long, hard kiss he normally reserved for New Year's Eve, or every Saturday morning before sex. When he broke the kiss, she was breathless and lightheaded.

"Wow."

"I probably could have waited on this until you got back, but maybe it'll give you that much more incentive to return safely."

"What are you talking about?"

James fumbled in the pocket of his khakis, then knelt before her. She covered her mouth in shock as he held up a small, red velvet box. Flipping it open, he presented her with the most beautiful art-deco style ring she'd ever seen.

"My GiGi gave this to me last year. She "saw" how we'd be together a long time, so told me I should propose with this."

"It's beautiful, James."

"So, will you? Marry me, I mean?"

"Of course!"

He smiled and pulled the ring from the box. As he slipped it on her finger, she felt a small jolt of electricity, like a static shock. He held the ring on her finger and blinked at her.

"Whoa."

"You felt it too?" she asked.

He nodded, then finally pushed the ring to the base of her finger. They laughed, and hugged, and kissed again. He held her against his chest, and she squeezed.

"You can bet your ass I'll get back safe now. I want the satisfaction of showing off this beauty."

"Hey!"

"Oh, and you, too, honey."

He smoothed his hand across her cheek, and gave her another quick kiss.

"All right. Go be a pioneer, Mar. I'll be right here in three days. If you don't show up, I'm calling every military branch, police station, and fire truck in the tri-state area to go in after you. Am I clear?"

She saluted, and he nodded in satisfaction.

"Go. Before I change my mind, and carry you off like a Neanderthal."

"I love you, James."

"I love you, too, Mary."

She hitched the backpack up on her shoulders, tightening the waist straps to secure it. Waving, she turned, then stepped over the rusted chain that sagged across the road. She gave one last look at the decrepit sign and marched forward, already anticipating what clues she might find in Cuthbert.

Three days later, as promised, James pulled the SUV up to the end of the main road into Cuthbert and parked close to the chain. He'd never seen Mar so excited about anything before, so he hoped she found what she was looking for.

Shutting off the engine, he exited the vehicle and walked around to the back. He popped open the tailgate, and prepped the picnic he'd brought. He figured she'd be needing a decent meal after three days of portable food. He could only assume because she had begged him the week prior *not* to call her at all hours to check in. If she needed help, she'd call him first.

He checked his watch. 11:30 a.m., exactly three days to the minute since he'd dropped her off. He couldn't honestly expect her to be standing here, but James was so anxious to see her. Three days had felt like three months.

At 11:45, he started to worry. Logically, he knew it was too early, but something in his gut refused to listen. He paced alongside the car, staring down the road toward Cuthbert. If she didn't come walking down that road in the next fifteen minutes, he'd go in after her.

At 12:07, he'd had enough. He closed the liftgate, grabbed his wallet and cell phone from the front seat, locked the car, then started walking to town. Mumbling to himself, he tried to focus on his receding anger, and not his growing fear.

"Why does she always have to do this? I don't care how much of a wilderness queen she thinks she is. She can't anticipate everything. *You can't anticipate everything Mar!*" he shouted into the surrounding trees.

As he envisioned her either so deep into her investigation she'd forgotten the day, OR, broken and trapped in a ravine, her SAT phone shattered in a dozen pieces next to her, he spotted a pile of leaves on the road ahead. He felt the need to charge through it, kicking and flailing to get rid of his growing panic.

Suddenly, it moved, and he stopped. Watching it closely, he feared it might be a wild animal, and not leaves at all. He wasn't prepared for a coyote or bobcat encounter. When the pile moved again, a section of it lifted. Two bloodshot eyes stared out at him.

"Holy shit, Mary!"

He ran to her, falling to his knees, and scooping her up. She moaned as he turned her to face him. Dirt and leaves matted her hair and clothing. Her face was covered in bloody scratches, some still wet and oozing. Her hands were raw and bleeding, as if she's gone ten rounds with a prize fighter. She croaked one sentence before passing out.

"Am I alive?"

Mary Ellen floated in darkness. It wasn't uncomfortable by any means, but somehow she knew she didn't belong here. Almost the second she decided to find her way out, a light appeared ahead of her. She heard muffled beeps, a whoosh, then what sounded like voices. The closer she got to the light, the clearer the sound became, until she could feel her body, heavy and sore. She struggled to open her eyes. Her arms felt as if they were encased in cement, but she managed to raise her hand to her face and swipe it across her brow.

"Mar?"

James' voice washed over her, and she finally opened her eyes. It took a minute to focus but when she could, she saw James standing over her, his face a wrinkled map of worry. She opened her mouth to reply, and her tongue caressed the plastic breathing tube stuck down her throat. Her gag reflex kicked in and she started to cough. James had already hit the call button, and a nurse rushed in before Mary Ellen could panic.

She removed the tube, speaking calmly. "You're okay. It's all right. I got it."

Once the tube was out, Mary Ellen coughed a few times and tried to speak again. A harsh rasp was all she could manage, and the nurse held a straw, inside a cup of water, to her lips.

"Here, take some water. Just sip it. Easy, there you go."

Mary Ellen managed not to choke while she swallowed, the cool water soothing her raw throat. As the nurse put the cup back on the side table, Mary Ellen smiled at James.

He grabbed her hand and squeezed. "You're gonna be okay, Mar."

She tried to talk again, but he shook his head. "Just rest. We can talk later, when you're feeling better."

She nodded, then stared at the nurse who checked her pulse and blood pressure. She smiled at Mary Ellen.

"I'll get the doctor, have him give you a once over, would that be all right?"

Mary Ellen nodded. The doctor came in minutes later,

checked her vitals, offered generic reassurances, then left. She was glad. She just wanted to sleep.

The image of a bloodied and torn corpse, hanging from an old knobby tree, flashed through her mind when she closed her eyes. They flew open, and she moaned. James bent down, still squeezing her hand.

"Mar, are you in pain?"

She shook her head, and took a few slow, deep breaths. She closed her eyes again, and another image popped up – a woman dressed in filthy, torn clothes, clutching a mangled pile of rags in her arms, as she ran down the middle of a muddy road. Mary Ellen's eyes flew open again, and she mewled, the remembered sorrow, pain, and anger flooding her brain.

James gripped her shoulders. "Should I call the doctor?"

"The doctor can't help her, Jamie."

Mary Ellen turned her head to look at GiGi as she approached the bed, a string of deep, black-colored stones clutched in her right hand. She scooched James away and took his place, gripping Mary Ellen's hand in her own, and wrapping the string around both. Mary Ellen looked at her, the older woman's eyes shining with pity, and Mary Ellen began to cry. She gripped GiGi's hand, reaching her left arm across her body to clutch at the woman's wrist. Tears spilled down both their faces, and Mary Ellen whispered.

"I'm so sorry. I didn't know... I didn't believe."

"Sshhh, hon. It's all right. I knew you'd have to learn it on your own. I just hoped it wasn't like this."

Mary Ellen wept. James stood off to the side, watching the two women comfort each other. Mar tried to smile, and reached out to him. He gripped her hand as his eyes misted over.

"Explain later. Need sleep. Drugs?" Mar whispered.

"You want me to see if the doctor will give you something to help you sleep?"

She nodded, and he ran out into the hall in search of the nurses' station. She looked back at GiGi, who reached down and wiped the tears from her face.

"The drugs will help for now. But you're going to have to face the reality of your experiences out there sooner or later."

Mary Ellen nodded, grateful for GiGi's presence. She was so foolish to have ignored the older woman's warnings about Cuthbert. But she couldn't face the horror right now. She just wanted to sleep and forget. For a little while, anyway.

Two days later, she was released from the hospital. James brought her home, where he had prepared their bedroom with a ton of fluffy pillows, loaded the cabinets with her favorite snack foods, and piled all her favorite DVDs into a storage bin next to the couch. As he held the door open for her, he babbled nervously.

"I've got every comfort you could ever want. And if it's not here, I'm happy to go get it for you. All you need to do is ask."

"Thank you, James. Really, you didn't have to do all this."

"Yes, I did. Now you go into the bedroom and get some rest. If you wanna talk – "

"Not right now. I just feel like crashing. Maybe in the morning. Would that be okay?"

He pulled her into a tight embrace, and she breathed in his scent, her raw nerves feeling soothed for the first time since she went to that damned town.

"Absolutely," he said. "Do you want anything specific to eat later?"

"We'll see how I feel. Thanks again."

He put her to bed, and she immediately fell into a fitful sleep. She woke the next morning to the smell of coffee and French toast. Slipping out from under the comforter, Mary Ellen shuffled to the kitchen. She sat on a stool next to the cut-out between the kitchen and the living room as she watched James bustle around, preparing breakfast. He hadn't heard her leave the bedroom, so when he turned and saw her, he jumped.

"Holy cats, Mar. You scared me."

"Sorry, I didn't want to interrupt."

He laughed and placed an empty mug in front of her. "Coffee?"

"Naturally."

He poured her a cup, then finished making their breakfast while she sipped the hot beverage. They ate in silence, but it was comfortable, like it always was before her nightmare adventure. After clearing away their dishes, James poured her some more coffee, then sat on a stool on one side of the cut-out, and she on the other. He stared at her over his mug.

"Do you think you might wanna talk about it?"

She studied her coffee and realized she did. She *needed* to talk about it because keeping it all inside was killing her. The nightmares, the fear – she thought they would take over and paralyze her for life. If anyone would understand, or at the very least be supportive, it was James.

She nodded. "I'm ready. I just hope you are, too."

"Hit me," he said as she began to recall the events of her days in Cuthbert.

Mary Ellen waved good-bye to James as she moved down

the road leading into Cuthbert. She heard him pull away and smiled. She loved James, but sometimes he could be so over protective, so stifling. Now, out here alone, she could enjoy the fresh air and sun, and concentrate on the task ahead. In just under an hour, she reached the center of town.

Shrugging the pack off her back, Mary Ellen studied the collection of worn store fronts, a small church, and a crumbling well in the center of town. Though the last population of ninety-eight people abandoned Cuthbert roughly twenty years ago, the whole town had the feel of its nineteenth century beginnings. She dug into an outer pocket of the pack and pulled out a city map.

The most recent one she could find was dated 1962, and the only thing missing from the blueprint was the stone well. Though a bit odd, it was possible the well was built after the plans had been completed. Once the town was abandoned in the late 1990s, it made sense that no one had bothered to update the files.

Mary Ellen folded the map, then dug into another pocket. Retrieving her wallet, she opened the side zipper, and pulled out a quarter. Loosely closing her fingers around it, she shook her hand, like she was about to throw a pair of dice in a craps game, and approached the well.

As she stood next to it, looking over the low wall into a dark and waterless shaft, Mary Ellen made a wish. "Please let me find something here."

Smiling, she tossed the quarter down, and heard the soft "plink" as it hit bottom. She closed her eyes and tilted her head, waiting for...well, she didn't know for sure, but some kind of sign to show her wish had come true.

All remained quiet, though, save for a soft breeze out of the west. She shrugged, laughing at herself, then walked back to her pack and the map. As she bent to grab the map, a shriek echoed all around her. Standing, she scanned the area, hoping to pinpoint its direction. It came again, a long agonizing scream filled with pain and horror, but Mary Ellen still couldn't figure out where it originated.

A flash of movement, something dark and fast, moved off to her right. She turned toward it, catching just a hint of it as it rushed between a small quilt shop and dentist office. Running forward, she called out.

"Hey, wait!"

Mary Ellen reached the storefront in seconds but when she looked down the alley, it lay empty.

"Hello?"

No response. Mary Ellen walked a few paces into the shaded alley when the cry sounded again from behind her. She whipped around, and ran back to the street. The dark shape entered the empty candy store across the way, and Mary Ellen ran toward it.

Bursting through the front door, she expected to catch the figure this time, but again, it was no where in sight. The layers of dirt, dust, and neglect sat untouched, the stale smell of abandonment wafted around her.

"What the hell?"

When she heard the shriek again, Mary Ellen tiptoed to the grimy front window, and stared out into the town. Back by the well, she spotted the fuzzy outline of the dark shape. Spitting into her hand, she cleaned a small section of the glass to get a clearer view of the street. The form hovered over her pack.

"Oh, shit."

Mary Ellen burst out of candy shop just in time to see her pack lifted off the ground. Though she originally thought the dark shape seemed formless because she only caught a glimpse of it, it truly was an amorphous black blob. It looked like it was testing the weight of her pack, and she charged forward, her fear of the thing less than her fear of being stuck out here without supplies for the next three days.

"Get away from that!"

It formed a humanoid figure, and looked up at her, surprised. It lifted the bag again, but Mary Ellen leaped at it, crashing her full 137 pounds on top of the pack, and they both slammed to the ground. The shape howled but flew off into the town and disappeared.

As she lay panting on the ground, Mary Ellen stared after it. "What the hell *was* that?"

She quickly sat up, and rifled through her pack. None of her supplies appeared to be missing, and she breathed a sigh of relief. The map nearly blew away on the breeze before she grabbed it. Immediately, she could feel something different. The paper felt thicker, softer from years of wear. She stared at the yellowed map. It looked old, like a relic from last century, though she had just made a copy of it a few weeks ago.

Mary Ellen took her time to unfold it, holding the edges between her thumb and forefinger so as not to handle it too roughly. When finished, the city map of Cuthbert, MI, *the 1859 plans*, lay before her.

"What the..."

The loud clank of a blacksmith's hammer against an anvil jerked her attention away from the paper. The ghostly figure of a large hulking man, with black apron and sweaty brow standing over a hot piece of steel, shimmered under the awning of the corner smithy shop. He faded almost as quickly as he appeared.

The crack of a horse whip brought Mary Ellen's

attention down the street as an open wagon pulled by two horses, its driver's hand raised in mid-lash, rolled away from her. It, too, disappeared.

As she watched, an entire city scape, straight from late nineteenth century, opened before her. Men and women walked along the wooden sidewalks or in the street; piano music from the local saloon floated on the afternoon breeze; carriages and wagons thumped along the rutted dirt road.

The shriek came again. The movement from the town stopped, as if it were all a projected image from a DVD, and someone hit "pause." Mary Ellen expected to see the shadow again but instead, a lone woman, clutching something against her chest, ran down the street.

Before Mary Ellen could stand, a mob of men carrying various tools, blunt and sharp objects, ran down the street following the woman. They shouted, encouraging each other to keep up and go after her, and Mary Ellen thought she heard a man yell, "demon." She watched them run past, disappearing around the corner of the blacksmith shop. She quickly threw her pack on her shoulders, clutching the map in one hand, and ran after them.

By the time she reached the corner, they had all disappeared. She stood in the middle of the dusty, empty road, scratching her head in puzzlement. The wind kicked up, and she heard a soft creak, like the hinges of an old door being opened after decades of neglect. She twisted her head left and right, but couldn't determine the source. It came again on another strong breeze, and her gaze fell on the giant oak tree at the end of the street.

She forced her feet to move, to take her over to the tree and the fragile object that hung from it. Mary Ellen already knew what it was, deep down she knew, but her mind wouldn't accept it. It felt like it took hours to walk those three short blocks, though it was most likely only minutes. When she reached the end, and stood before the massive tree, Mary Ellen closed her eyes, and took a long, deep breath.

When she opened them, she tilted her head back and stared up at the tattered remains of the woman she'd just seen running through the town followed by an angry mob of grown men. Her arms hung slack at her side, her tongue poking out through cracked lips. Her bare feet, cut and still bleeding, swung side to side. The creak of the thick rope floated on the air. Mary Ellen hung her head, wiping a hand across her face.

"What is going on?"

She then noticed a small lump sitting on the ground beneath the hanging woman. It must be what she'd been carrying. Mary Ellen bent down, and gently pulled at a corner of the torn blanket that was caked with mud, and stiff with dried blood. Opening the lumpy package, Mary Ellen fell back in horror, scrabbling away from the mangled remains of a newborn baby.

The sudden cries of dozens of townsfolk surrounded her. She looked through a sea of dust coated slacks and skirts, rough leather work boots, and pointed heels. Mary Ellen stared up at the gathering of people. They paid her no attention as they lifted their torches and voices in unison.

"Demon whore!"

One woman, near the front of the group, stepped forward and spat at the swinging body. Another kicked dirt on the dead child. Soon, the entire mob rushed forward, swinging their clubs at the woman like a piñata, while others stomped and trampled the infant remains until there was nothing left but a thick slurry of blood soaking into the dry ground.

When they'd all had their fill, they abandoned their bloodlust at the base of the tree, turned, and left the scene. Each person faded as they moved farther away, back to their own time and long-dead memories. The woman and her baby had also disappeared, but Mary Ellen couldn't wipe their images from her brain, and she promptly rolled onto her hands and knees, and vomited into the dirt.

As the heaving slowed, and her stomach emptied, she sat back on her heels, wiping her mouth, and wondered what she'd gotten herself into.

That night she decided to sleep in the abandoned corner store, where she'd seen the vision of the long-ago blacksmith hammering away at his wares. The weather was clear and warm, but she didn't trust sleeping outside, exposed and vulnerable. Not with that dark mass flitting about, or the visions she'd had about the townspeople.

She felt a small sense of protection from the empty structure, and it should suffice as a decent shelter until the morning when she planned to get the hell out of here, thesis be damned. Mary Ellen snuggled into her sleeping bag, the battery lamp next to her head, while she studied the old map that had somehow ended up in her possession.

The edges of the paper were fuzzy and worn, but the plans themselves, the building layouts, the street names, every detail down to the multiple hitching posts placed about the town, remained clear and sharp, as if they'd just been drawn up yesterday. The differences between this map, and the one she'd gotten from the city, were the red and blue, horizontal and perpendicular lines marking the Hartman Curry grid that crisscrossed over the paper, and the missing well.

She dug through her pack, and found the original map she'd picked up weeks ago. She laid it over the old map.

Using her fingers as a rough measuring guide, she noted the well sat in the exact center of town over one point where four of the colored lines intersected. The other areas where any of the lines crossed were the candy shop and the oak tree, and each of those showed only two lines intersecting.

Mary Ellen remembered a snippet of the conversation she'd had with GiGi months ago after telling the older woman about her thesis. She'd never prescribed to GiGi's new-agey bullshit but she couldn't deny an eerie similarity to this map and what GiGi had told her.

"You can't go to Cuthbert," GiGi said.

Mary Ellen pinched the bridge of her nose and sighed. "And why's that?"

"Too much bad energy surrounding it. There's a reason it was abandoned, why nothing and no one could flourish there."

"Bad juju?" Mary Ellen snorted.

"I know you think I'm a big joke, missy, but it's been scientifically *proven that the world is covered with criss-crossing lines of good and bad energy. And when those energies transect, you can get something either fantastic, or monstrous."*

Mary Ellen sat up and peeked out of the blacksmith's window. The black, swirling creature hovered near the door of the candy shop, and Mary Ellen quickly ducked back down. She stared at the old map. Grabbing a pen from her pack, she circled the candy store, the tree, and the well. She'd already seen horror at the tree. And though not much else happened today, she didn't exactly want to run over to the candy shop and snoop around.

That left the well. She hadn't seen anything horrific there, except when the creature tried to get her backpack. But otherwise, it seemed rather innocuous. She didn't know if that was more, or less, worrisome. If the oak tree, where she'd witnessed the most horrific event of her life so far, had two lines of energy crossing at its location, what did four lines mean? What awaited at the well?

She tucked both maps back into her pack, buried her entire body inside her sleeping bag, and prayed for morning. She didn't expect to get much sleep, but after a few hours of analyzing every little bump and scrape she heard, her weary mind and body finally fell into a restless slumber.

The crowing of a rooster jarred her awake. Mary Ellen bolted up, holding her fists in front of her face, ready to defend herself. When nothing immediately attacked her, she relaxed and looked around. The rooster crowed again, and she slowly peeked over the ledge of the front window. The proud, fat bird perched on the lip of the well and crowed a third time. A rotund man, in dirty coveralls and a wide brimmed hat, swiped at the rooster, then wrapped it up in one of his thick arms. It protested for a moment, but soon relaxed as he stuck it in an open cage in the bed of his rusty pick-up truck. A young woman, dressed in a sack dress and worn saddle shoes, hopped down from the passenger seat. Once the man had locked the bird up, he turned to her, and threw a back-handed swing across her face. She crumpled to the ground, a slight cry of surprise escaped her as she hit the packed dirt.

Mary Ellen scrabbled out of her sleeping bag, and burst out of the blacksmith shop, hopping as she pulled on her boots.

"Hey! What the hell do you think you're doing?"

The couple paid her no attention. The man stood over the weeping woman, his face red with anger.

"Do you know how much we would have lost at the market if that damned rooster got away? How many times – "

He kicked her in the shin. "Do I have to tell you – "

He kicked her in the ribs. "To make sure those damn birds are secure?"

His dirty boot connected with her jaw and sent her reeling. She rolled once, landing facedown on the street, and didn't move. He kicked her two more times before he stood back, pulled a stained handkerchief from his back pocket, and wiped the sweat from his face. Mary Ellen lurched toward him, ready to scratch his eyes from their sockets, but she flew right through him, and sprawled to the ground. Their images faded, and she was alone in the street. She twisted left and right, but the couple and their truck were gone. The wind whipped up, whistling through the empty buildings and alleys, moaning like a trapped ghost in a long-forgotten home.

Closing her eyes, Mary Ellen took several long, deep breaths.

"Get a grip, Mar. You're hallucinating. Just like the hanging, the crowd, probably even that thing flying around. None of this is real."

She didn't know if that was good or bad. But she managed to convince herself that everything would be fine once she had some coffee and food. After finishing breakfast, while she cleaned up her supplies, a ghastly shriek pierced the morning air. Mary Ellen clutched the zippered pack filled with coffee grounds, and squeezed her eyes closed.

"It's not real. None of this is real."

A shadow passed over her, blocking the sun streaming through the front window, and she opened her eyes. The shape, the one she'd seen swooping about the town, hovered before her. She gasped. It grabbed her by the hair, and dragged her out into the street.

As the dust settled around her, she saw the woman, clutching her baby, run screaming around the corner, followed by a group of people. The large man in his dirty coveralls kicked an unconscious woman lying next to his truck. A group of young teens battered an elderly woman with baseball bats and stones over by the candy shop, her white gloves stained with blood while their bellbottoms flapped around her. A half-dozen more acts of violence swam in and out of focus, snippets of time on an infinite loop, trapped in this no-where town.

Mary Ellen scooched against the low stone wall of the well, clapping her hands over her ears, trying to block out the screams and the low thumps of fist or foot against soft flesh. The cacophony swirled around her, and she could feel it vibrating in her bones. Just as it became too much, just as she started to scream in helpless agony, it stopped.

She slowly opened her eyes and the street, the entire town, lay empty. Mary Ellen swiveled her head back and forth, and heard nothing but blessed silence. But the dark shape floated just a few feet away. It slowly moved toward her. Paralyzed with fear, she could do nothing but watch its approach. It quickly darted to the left, taking one full spin around the well, then stopped at her side, its black countenance inches from her face.

It formed what looked like an arm, and extended it toward her. It pointed at her, then the well, then back to her. She looked between the two, confused. Remembering when she first arrived (was it only yesterday?), throwing the quarter down the well and making a wish, she felt her eyes widen as she stared back at the dark shape.

A low chuckle, like the thunder of an approaching storm, filled her ears. It was laughing at her. Shaking her head, she scrambled to her feet, and ran back to the blacksmith's shop, the fiend's laughter growing until it filled the entire town with its malevolence. She slid into the shop, and crouched behind the front window, breathing heavy. The sounds returned – the screaming, the beatings – but they seemed a bit muffled from inside her hiding place.

She knew she couldn't stay there forever. That thing would eventually get her, and she would become a part of the tortured history of this place. If she could just get out of the town, beyond the city's limits, Mary Ellen believed she would be safe. She had no proof, of course, but it was her only plan right now. She jammed her belongings into the pack, and secured it to her back. Taking another peek over the window sill, she didn't see the dark creature anywhere, just the general mayhem of violence past.

Crawling to the door, she checked every angle of the street that she could as she peeked through the opening. Still not seeing the thing, Mary Ellen leaped to her feet, and darted out the door, turning right and heading north toward the outskirts of town. She had to run past the well before hitting the main road, but aside from the phantom of a young man strangling his twin to death before throwing him down the stone structure, all was quiet.

As she reached the corner where a small, worn-down church sat, something grabbed her from behind. The pack strained against her shoulders as she was thrown to the ground, landing on her ass with a heavy thud. The hard-packed earth jarred her bones, and gravel tore up the backs of her legs. The dark shape hovered over her, inching closer as she inched away, herding her back toward the middle of town. The closer the shadow moved toward the well, the stronger it seemed to get.

She jumped up and darted left, hopping to run around the church, or one of the smaller stores, and get back to the main road. It grabbed her again, and threw her toward the well. This time she seemed to fly through the air, her body suspended above the ground for what felt like minutes before she slammed against the road. The air left her lungs in one big whoosh, and she couldn't move.

The thing stayed just out of reach as it watched her. Satisfied she wasn't able to run away again, it disappeared. Mary Ellen lay on her back for several minutes as she tried to catch her breath. When she felt her heart wouldn't explode from lack of oxygen, she rolled over, shrugging the pack off, and stood on wobbly legs.

She staggered to the shelter of the blacksmith shop, and collapsed just inside the door. After resting for several minutes, she rolled over onto her stomach, and peeked out at the street. She'd left the pack laying in the middle of the road, near the well. The supplies she'd need to survive the next two days, before James showed up, were in there. She needed to get it back.

Mary Ellen crawled on her belly toward the pack, swiveling her head back and forth, keeping a wary eye open for the creature's return. Just as she reached it, a howling shriek sounded from her left. On the other side of town, the shadow flew toward her. She jumped to her feet, snagging the pack as she turned to run. It caught her from behind and slammed her to the ground. The pack rolled away but she and the creature grabbed it at the same time.

Pulling against one another, the pack tore open, her

supplies scattering across the dirt. She managed to grab a bottle of water and a protein bar before scuttling back to the safety of the blacksmith's shop. The shadow dumped the pack, and the remainder of her supplies, down the well. She stared at the measly bottle and foil wrapped snack in her hands, and prayed it would be enough.

Over the next two days, she and the creature played cat and mouse. If she tried to venture outside the shop, or too far from the well, the creature would attack, leaving her bruised and bloody. Sometimes, she would be forced to watch the atrocities stuck in time, like she witnessed the first day she arrived, as warnings of her possible fate. It kept her scared and weak, and the single bottle of water and protein bar she'd managed to snag, were barely enough to sustain her.

On the third day, Mary Ellen decided to risk it all. She couldn't allow herself to die, huddled and alone, terrified, never to be found again. She tilted the empty bottle back, a single gulp of water soaking into her parched tongue, then threw it to the side. She stood, her weakened legs shaky and unsteady, but after a few deep breaths, she worked up the courage to move forward. She shuffled out into the street. The creature was nowhere to be found.

A car, circa 1950, sped past her. She could feel the rush of air as it passed, the small stones kicked up by the body being dragged from the car's bumper, bounced off her legs. The other horrible visions had been just that – visions. No substance, no matter. This time, she'd felt it. The longer she remained here, the more a part of the town she became.

"Fuck that noise," she whispered, her voice cracking.

Summoning up the last of her strength, she bolted down the main road. She'd run nearly a mile before the horrible screech of the dark creature sounded from behind her.

Twisting her body as she ran, she could see a blurry figure behind the candy shop. Mary Ellen darted to her left, past a giant maple tree, and dove into the woods along the main road.

Pressing her back against the tree, she took a minute to catch her breath and listen. The shrieking creature was still behind her, but not as close as she'd thought. She dared a peek around the trunk, and saw the shape swirling and flying around the well. Her theory of it being the shadow's source was correct – and the farther away it moved from the structure, the weaker it became. Which meant Mary Ellen now had something she'd been without for two days: hope.

A horse and buggy raced past her, a woman chopping a small hatchet into the driver's neck, then quickly faded. An old man in sagging, worn pants and rough, cloth shirt, stumbled as a trio of young boys stoned him. A wild-haired woman cut open the belly of a young pregnant girl as she lay in the grass at Mary Ellen's feet. She clamped a hand over her mouth to keep from screaming as this vision, too, faded.

These horrors popped up all around her, but Mary Ellen remained quiet. A shriek of frustration came from the creature at the well, and she chanced another look. It turned away from her direction and flew toward the back part of town, where the old oak tree stood. Since it hadn't found her hiding place, it went to search elsewhere.

She quietly moved through the underbrush, each step slow and painful as prickers and half-dead branches scratched her legs, but she managed to get to the road without making too much noise. Half-jogging, Mary Ellen proceeded forward. She knew the end of the road wasn't far away, where James would soon arrive, and she could get the hell out of here.

Perhaps the close end to this nightmare allowed her body to relax, to suspend the flow of adrenalin. Her legs trembled and buckled beneath her. She slumped to the ground, resting her head on her arms, and breathed heavily. As her body let go of the past three days of fear and tension, she almost fell asleep. But the creature's far away screeching snapped her back to reality. It wasn't quite over yet.

She crawled forward, clawing hand over hand. She couldn't be sure, but it sounded like the creature was getting closer, though she knew it would be weakened this far from the well. She scrabbled at a pile of leaves and twigs on her left, pushing them across her legs and up over her body, hoping to evade detection.

She didn't know how long she lay there. She may have passed out. But the sound of approaching footsteps roused her, and she risked lifting her head to look. James stood staring at her, his eyes wide in horror.

"Holy shit, Mary!"

He ran to her, and scooped her up in his arms. Her entire body ached with the movement and fear tingled the back of her neck as she stared up at him. Could this be real?

"Am I alive?" she asked before blackness consumed her.

James sat across from her at the breakfast nook, his expression one of shock and horror. She worried he might think her crazy, and send her back to the hospital.

"I swear, I'm not making any of this up."

He grabbed her hand. "Oh, I know that, Mar. I wasn't thinking that at all."

She gripped his hand and smiled with relief. "Thank you. Now, I just don't know where to go from here. What do I do with all this?"

"Are you still thinking about your thesis?"

She nodded. "Mm-hmm. There's gotta be a way I can work this into my paper, but how?"

"I think you've got a bigger problem than that, Mar."

"Like what?"

He slipped off his stool, and stepped away from her. He nodded at something just over her shoulder. The cold fear of the past week enveloped her heart as she slowly turned around.

The black shadow, the creature that had tormented her in the abandoned town, floated in the living room. She leaped from her stool and it clattered to the floor. Pressing herself against the low counter at her back, Mary Ellen trembled and shook her head.

"That's impossible. It can't be here. It can't be away from the well."

"It's not here, Mar."

She spun to look at James, and saw the cruel smile on his face. Suddenly, he placed his hands on the counter, and thrust his face toward hers. Blackness swirled in his eyes, and the deep, throaty laughter of a beast from the depths of an unending abyss, echoed through the apartment.

"You'll never leave. You'll never be free again."

The clean walls of the apartment wavered and eventually faded, and the dusty wooden structure of the blacksmith's shack rose around her. A wave of dizziness crashed down, and she fell to the floor. Her pack lay on her right, the edges of the two maps peeking out of a pocket, and her sleeping bag on the left. The sun streamed through the front window, and the crowing of a rooster floated on the morning breeze.

"No. No. Nonononononono."

She jumped to her feet and looked out the window. A

heavy-set man picked up the rooster and it quieted. After depositing it into a cage in the open bed of a rusted pickup truck, he backhanded a young woman across the face, and she crumpled to the ground. While he kicked her, as she curled up into a ball, Mary Ellen ran out into the street.

"Hey! What the hell do you think...you're..."

She stopped halfway to the truck, watching the man as he beat the woman unconscious. Within minutes, the figures faded as other images of people, dressed in clothing from various decades, flashed in and out through the town. She fell to her knees, the small stones of the dirty road digging into her skin.

The shadow creature floated in circles around her several times before it lowered itself directly in front of her. It formed blurry shapes that resembled a face, and it flashed a vague, toothy smile at her.

"You're mine now, Mary Ellen. Forever."

LONG

Jim and Brian sat on the low wall of the dry, stone well. The heat of the mid-summer day kept them out of the fields and, finally tiring of playing in the barn, the two boys stared into the dark shaft.

"How far down do you think it goes?" Brian asked.

Jim leaned over the hole. "I bet all the way to China. That's what Robbie said."

"Your brother's an idiot. It can't go all the way to China."

"I guess there's only way to find out. Throw something down there."

Brian stared at his friend. "Like what?"

Jim stepped behind Brian, bent down, then grabbed the boy's ankles. Brian laughed, but his voice shook with uncertainty.

"Hey, Jim. What are you doing? Stop kidding arou-"

Jim stood, and threw all ninety-two pounds of his body weight into lifting Brian up and over the wall. The boy screamed as he tumbled into the darkness. Several thuds, and one loud crash later, Jim scratched his head.

"Huh. I guess Robbie *was* wrong."

From the far side of the field, Jim could see his mother standing on the porch of their farmhouse. She waved her arms, and he mirrored her. He picked up a heavy stone, and threw it into the well. It bounced off the shaft walls, and landed with a hearty "squish" at the bottom. He brushed the dirt from his hands, and started the long trek back to the house.

RAPTCHAARRR!

Captain Redbone stood in the fighting top of the main mast, a spyglass at his eye, and the sun at his back. The crisp, white sails billowed around him as the wind pushed the *Golden Maiden* forward. Well, maybe not so much crisp or white as worn and dirty, but they served their purpose all the same. The state of the ship's sails were the least of his concerns right now. If the storm ahead was as violent on the water as it was in the sky, the semantics on the condition of the *Maiden*'s sails wouldn't matter if she ended up at the bottom of the sea.

Black and green clouds swirled above the surface of the ocean. Arcs of lightening broke across the thunderheads, sparking like a flame on the spilled remnants of a powder keg. Though still miles away, the storm seemed to approach the *Maiden*, not the other way around. The Captain had never seen such a display in all his years upon the water. He'd lived through hurricanes in Jamaica, cyclones near the tip of Gibraltar, and water devils that spit and hissed promises of doom on any ship that dared pass too close.

But he had never seen the likes of what lay ahead. It looked like...

"It's the end of the world, Captain!"

Redbone looked at the deck below to see the quartermaster, Robin Marks. The man, nearly five feet tall and almost as wide, called through his thick calloused hands.

"It's the end!"

The Captain compressed the spyglass against his thigh, and tucked it into his coat pocket. He grabbed the nearest rope and swung down, taking one spin around the mast before dropping the last few feet to the deck. Marks took the line from Redbone's hands, and the Captain noted his shipmate's trembling shoulders.

"What are you on about, Marks?"

"It's the end of the–"

"World, yes. You said that already."

"Don't you see, Cap'n? Just like the legends tell us."

"You're going to have to be a bit more specific, Marks. Which legends?"

"You know, *the* legends. The tales of how one day the seas will be swallowed whole by the God of all that is because he's unhappy with us."

"And us being...?"

"Humans, sir! God don't like the way we humans is mucking up the world!"

Redbone wriggled a finger under his bandana and scratched absently at his scalp. "Why, Marks. I never knew you were the religious type."

"Don't poke fun, sir. It's bad luck."

The Captain could almost see his own eyes as they rolled back in an expression of exasperation.

"Everything is bad luck to you, Marks. Spitting on

Sundays, twitching your nose on Thursdays, using your left hand on Fridays. Honestly, man, what isn't bad luck to you?"

Marks seemed to think about it. He opened his mouth to respond only to snap it closed and continued thinking. Redbone laughed, and moved toward the bow. He wanted to take another look at the impending squall. As he walked, Marks followed behind, blathering on about "The End."

"It's true I ain't never read the Bible or been known to be regular about any church. But I wasn't always a lover of piracy, sir. I had me a mother once, and she'd read to me about God and all that."

"And I assume you'll be telling me the lessons she passed on to you?"

"Yes, sir."

"I don't suppose I could stop you, could I?"

"No, sir."

Redbone laughed again. "Then by all means, Mr. Marks. Do tell. What did her Bible say about the end of the world?"

Before the quartermaster could speak, the ship heaved. The mermaid figurehead rose into the sky. Every man standing on the deck was thrown onto his back. The few unfortunate crew members climbing the shrouds were flung free to sail through the air, and either break against one of the heavy timbered masts or go over the side and into the dark water.

"What the devil?"

Captain Redbone staggered to his feet, and grabbed one of the chains along the gangway. He could see the kerchiefed heads of two of his crew just before they sank below the now churning waves. Only moments ago, the water lay still, the violence of the approaching storm too far away to affect them yet. But he turned back to look over the bow, and what had been a distant storm was now a tempest in their midst.

The churning clouds were indistinguishable from the darkening sky. What looked like a whirlpool, but in the air not the water, spun before them. The blackness of a moonless, night sky rolled out from the hole, spreading from one end of the horizon to the other like a giant black sail. The sun, which had been above the ship, began to fall into that expanding darkness, its light and warmth quickly dying. The sound of a thousand sucking tide pools growled, coming from everywhere, and nowhere, at the same time, drowning out even the roaring thunder.

As the Captain shouted orders to the rest of the crew, the wind pushed against the ship with ferocious power, bringing it closer to the swirling brink. The sails stretched beyond their capacity, and began to tear. Several bowlines snapped. One lashed against a crewman, knocking him to the deck. The ship rolled again on a giant swell, and the man slid overboard, screaming and clawing for purchase until the ocean swallowed him.

Marks pulled the grey knit cap from his head and wrung it between his hands. He shouted above the cacophony of what looked to be the world collapsing in on itself.

"And the Heavens will open, and the blackness of all that isn't will swallow the world. Only the faithful, the true believers of God, will go to be with Him in His kingdom. The rest will fall into the void, and forever burn in the fiery pits of Hell!"

"Marks, you fool! Quit blathering and secure the downhaul! Reef those sails before–"

What sounded like a pistol shot echoed across the ship.

The crosstrees cracked, and the main mast began to sway in the wind. It rocked the ship fore and aft, starboard to port. Redbone struggled to stay on his feet as he made his way to throttle Marks, just to keep him quiet.

"Oh, Captain! I don't want to die and go to Hell!"

Redbone grabbed the quartermaster by the front of his shirt.

"Marks, whether you go to Heaven or Hell is between you and your God. But you will die, by my hands sooner than this maelstrom, if you continue to blather and moan like a briny wench. Move!"

Marks scuttled away and grabbed the nearest bitt with one hand, reached for a flailing line with the other, then secured it in place. His deep sense of duty to the ship and his captain now taking precedence in his mind, Marks stopped moaning about the afterlife, and helped to secure the *Maiden*. Satisfied, Redbone turned to make his way to the bow. What he saw sent a chill across his skin.

The bowspirit had already entered the looming black. The Captain stood frozen on the main deck, unable to tear his eyes away from the nothingness that prepared to swallow the *Golden Maiden*, her crew, and the world. For a brief moment, Redbone felt a spike of fear pierce his heart. Were there pits of eternal flames waiting for him on the other side of that void? Because they favored piracy, and the pleasures of the flesh over matters of the spirit, would he and his brethren be forever doomed with pain and torture in the next world?

As the ship passed into the black depths, Captain Redbone closed his eyes and prepared himself for the worse pain he could imagine.

Nothing happened.

After several minutes of more nothing, Redbone opened

his eyes. He and the rest of his crew stood on the shores of a vast ocean. The white sands beneath their feet sparkled like jewels of a long-lost treasure; the rippling water before them shone as only the sea can when the sun casts its rays upon her face.

The Captain looked at Marks, who stood on his left. "Mr. Marks, me thinks your mother's Bible got it wrong."

Marks could only smile and nod as he stared at the glory around them. Soon the rest of the crew, even the mates that had been washed overboard, were laughing and clapping each other on their backs. So proud they were of themselves they hadn't noticed the tall, stately gentleman carrying a large scroll until after he cleared his throat.

"Excuse me, are you the men from the *Golden Maiden*?"

Captain Redbone stepped forward, and gave the man a grand bow. "I am the Captain of the *Maiden*. And you are?"

"Hobbs, sir. Randall Hobbs."

"Mr. Hobbs, can you tell me where we can find our ship?"

"Your ship, Captain? What do you mean?"

"Can't you see that great expanse of water there, man? Where is the *Maiden* so that we may be on our way?"

"Oh, I'm afraid the *Maiden* was lost. But not to worry. We have something much bigger in mind for all of you now. Please, follow me."

The Captain motioned for his men to follow, though he felt a slight flutter of panic in his chest. He tried not to show it, and instead focused on their surroundings. The glittering beach stretched out as far as he could see, and the ocean nestling against it reached the horizon like a perfect blue-green pane of glass. He noticed now the slight breeze brought no scent of salt or sea. The small ripples of water against the shore made no sound. The sun that hung above them provided no warmth.

Redbone tried to picture what kind of vessel they would get to sail that infinite sea. Though he was saddened by the loss of the *Maiden*, an exceptional and beautiful ship he'd won after cheating his way out of a bad game of cards, he imagined here they would be given an even finer vessel, one to rival all ships throughout the entire history of piracy.

As they left the beach and the water behind, the group of men crossed a narrow cobblestone street, then proceeded to a squat grey stone building. A small rectangular door sat in the middle of the wall, adorned by two small dirty windows on either side. Mr. Hobbs ducked through the doorway, and indicated they do the same. Redbone wasn't sure how Marks would fit through the slender opening, but once inside, the Captain forgot about his crewmates.

The dim, dusty room sprawled out beyond the length of his vision, for he could not see the opposite wall or the ceiling. What looked like a small jail from the outside appeared to be a warehouse of sorts that could have fit thousands of *Golden Maiden*s inside. The wooden planks of the floor lay cracked and weathered as if left to dry in the sun and turn to driftwood.

People. Hundreds, thousands, perhaps hundreds of thousands, stumbled around the vast space, tripping into and against each other. Barely enough room to change direction, most wandered on bleeding feet, torn to shreds by the rough wood beneath them. Still they walked. Their eyes vacant, soulless, empty, they neither heard nor felt nor saw the rest of the damned. Only their own bloody flesh mattered, scraping along the wooden floor with the clack of protruding bones, as they roamed this forsaken room.

"What is this place?" Marks asked.

"Nothing for you to worry about, Mr. Marks. But you," Hobbs pointed at three men behind the quartermaster. "You three remain here."

He shoved them away from the crew, and into the milling crowd where they quickly fell into step, almost as if they'd been here for centuries. Mr. Hobbs unrolled the parchment, and pulled a quill from behind his ear. He stuck the point into his wrist, dotting the end with blood, and made three check marks on the paper. Motioning to the rest of them, Hobbs continued forward.

"Follow me, please. The rest of you are assigned elsewhere."

"Assigned?" Redbone asked. "Assigned for what?"

Hobbs turned to look at him. "For your jobs in Hell, of course, Captain."

"But, where are the fires? The pit?" Marks asked.

Hobbs tsked at him. "Oh, really, Mr. Marks. Did you honestly think Hell was so simple? So mundane?"

"I–"

"Yes, I suppose you did. You must have read the Bible or whatever it's called. Human words written by human men. I guess they wouldn't have the savvy to describe it properly."

Mr. Hobbs began to chuckle. "Excuse my impertinence but did you see what I did there? 'Savvy?' While describing Hell to pirates?"

When the crew didn't laugh, Mr. Hobbs shrugged. "No one appreciates my sense of humor around here. Come along, gentlemen."

The men followed Mr. Hobbs from one immeasurable room to the next. At each one, Mr. Hobbs would cull several members of the group, and leave them to their eternal fates.

They reached a room which held rows and rows of wooden troughs similar to ones used to feed pigs.

Here the beasts that lined up for their feeding looked like humans who walked on hands and feet, hunched and filthy and savage as they jostled for position. Tall lumbering giants hauled wooden buckets heavy with bloody arms, legs, heads, and organs, then slopped the offal into the troughs. With growing horror, Redbone realized the creatures *were* men, damned to live and sup off the remains of human corpses.

Another area was dotted with hundreds of openings in the floor, each filled with a different dark and viscous fluid. Mud covered women used long wooden poles to push howling and crying men into the pits, forcing them to choke and drown. Afterwards, the women would reach down into the muck and pull the men free. Gasping for breath, they would return to life. Then the process would begin anew: shove, drown, revive; shove, drown, revive.

For years, the dwindling crew followed Mr. Hobbs through Hell's many rooms. Torture chambers, lava pools, a large melee of men and women dressed as rabbits hitting each other with pillows, suffocation dens, skinning tables, one oversized fire pit into which Marks was pushed, slabs of white marble where naked women covered in honey lay as Hobbs pulled the Captain forward before he could see anything more.

"Come along, Captain."

"Can we just go back to that room, or at least the rabbit one?"

"Your assignment is just ahead, sir. Please don't dawdle."

"But–"

"Ah, here we are!"

Redbone stumbled into Mr. Hobbs. He mumbled an apology, then stared at the wharf before them. The massive wooden structure stretched into a raging sea that churned under a hot yellow sun. The wind carried the scent of jasmine and spices to his nose. Moored to the massive dock was the largest and grandest ship Redbone had ever laid his eyes upon. It made the *Golden Maiden* look like a wobbly raft constructed of twigs and pine sap.

"What's this?"

"This is the ship that takes souls to Heaven."

"The ship that...You mean I'm going to Heaven?"

"Oh, goodness no, Captain. You? Now that is a joke."

Mr. Hobbs leaned his head back and cackled. After several hearty belly laughs, Hobbs bent forward and retched. A heap of pink and red glistening organs piled up at his feet. When the final loop of intestine slipped past his lips, he stood and wiped his mouth.

"Forgive me. I took pleasure in poisoning people during my lifetime, and now whenever I have a good laugh, I regurgitate my entrails."

Redbone grimaced. "Do you need to, uh, put them back in?"

"What? Oh, no. They've already reformed inside, ready to pop out the next time I'm amused."

"All right. So, what is my assignment?"

"It's the ferryman."

"Ferryman? I thought he brought people into the land of the dead. Aren't we already here?"

"Did you see a ferryman bring you over when you died?"

"No."

"Exactly. When you die, your soul automatically transports to Purgatory, that expanse of beach you saw outside. But the souls need to be ferried from there into Heaven."

"That was Purgatory? I thought Purgatory was–"

"What? A great expanse of fog? Blackness? Nothing? Honestly, you people really need to stop taking things so literally."

"Why aren't the souls ferried into Hell?"

"Really, Captain? You needed someone to transport you all the way across the street?"

"No, I suppose not, but then why isn't the ferry out there? Why make everyone walk through Hell?"

"What makes you think every soul that walks through the front door walks directly into Hell?"

The Captain opened his mouth to reply but found he had no answer to give.

"Good. May we proceed?"

Redbone nodded.

"Like I said, the ferryman–"

"Yes, you need me to be the ferryman, to take charge of this ship?"

"Please let me finish. We already have a ferryman. He told me that it's taking far too long for the souls to travel up that small path to the dock where they can board. They also tend to drag mud from the trail onto the ship. And with the apocalypse and the influx of new souls, there's no telling how much muck will be tracked over everything."

"What does this have to do with me?"

"We created a new position just for you, Captain. We need you to carry the souls along the path to the dock."

Redbone stared at Mr. Hobbs. "I beg your pardon?"

"What didn't you understand?"

"The whole thing."

Mr. Hobbs sighed, then led Captain Redbone by the

arm down a narrow muddy rut that had been dug by a small trickle of water through the surrounding marshy grasses. It twisted and turned until it ended at the edge of a dark forest. A line of people stood waiting behind a heavy chain. Hobbs pointed at the obese woman in front. He spoke slowly to Redbone as if to a dimwitted child.

"These people," he gestured with his hands, "need you," he pointed at the Captain, "to carry them," he hunched over pretending to walk with someone on his back, "to the ship."

He moved his hand through the air, mimicking the motion of a ship rolling on ocean waves, then pointed to the colossal boat sitting at the dock.

"You must be joking."

"Why?"

"Well, I was expecting something more like red hot irons stuck in my eyes, or being set on the rack and pulled apart day after day."

"You don't think this is severe enough punishment, Captain?"

"I suppose I don't."

"Let me ask you something. What was the best thing about being a pirate?"

The Captain turned to look at the ship, the water, the sun. He tilted back his head, closed his eyes, and took a deep breath.

"Nothing was more satisfying than sailing across the open water. The feel of wood beneath my feet – solid yet in constant motion. The flap of the sails as the ship breaks past the far edge of a rocky coastline before setting upon the unending sea. The sensation of–"

"Yes, freedom, wind in your sails, all that. I understand. But you seem to think that being burned with fire would be worse than staring up at this grand vessel, and never being able to board her."

Redbone opened his eyes. Hobbs continued.

"You think drowning in a pool of your own excrement would be worse than having to stare at wave upon wave of water, never again having the chance to feel that rocking rhythm under your feet."

The Captain's knees buckled, and he sank into the wet grass. It felt as though his heart had turned to marble.

"Evisceration, mutilation, torture, whippings, having to eat your own tongue day after day would be worse than carrying millions of souls to this ship, to their salvation, while you remain moored to land, and watch them disappear over the horizon? Forever leaving you to stand on the shore, alone?"

Captain Redbone wept into his hands. No, he could imagine no worse Hell for someone like him. He felt Mr. Hobbs grab his arms, and pull him up.

"No time for that, Captain. You've got work to do."

Hobbs unrolled the parchment again, and made one last checkmark in blood. He tucked the scroll under his arm, then moved to unhook the chain. The large woman at the head of the line walked up to the Captain. She stood before him, arms folded across her chest, waiting.

Redbone turned his back to her, and stared at the docked ship. He grimaced as the full weight of the burden settled on his back, and he began the first stumbling trek of his new eternity.

WHO'S THE MONSTER?

Phillip leaned over the edge of his bed. He poked Rashka's spit sac, and the monster screeched in pain. Phillip's mother rushed into the room, and pulled up the bed skirt.

"What happened, sweetie?"

The monster crawled out, and wrapped its six arms around her neck.

She stared at Phillip. "If you can't treat your Vonkep better, I'll have to return him to the shelter."

"Aw, mom."

As she left Phillip's room, gently caressing the creature in her arms, she looked back at her son. "Or maybe I'll just return you."

Phillip trembled under his covers as the door closed.

OFFERINGS

The scent of crisp apples perfumed the fall wind as it wafted under her nose. The unusual warmth of the air wrapped around her shoulders, but tickled the back of her neck with a cold, sharp undercurrent. A sudden gust took her by surprise, and she heard the faint cry of a car alarm in its wake. Her blonde hair whipped across her cheeks, but the binding ropes kept her arms pinned to her sides, denying her the ability to brush it away.

Unable to turn and watch the deepening violet of the night sky behind her, she stared at the sun as it dipped below the horizon. The fading layers of orange, yellow, and pink offered a sense of nostalgia, and a reminder of the inevitability that all things must end. As she tried to remember the last time she'd watched a sunset, a single crow flew across her line of sight.

Her heart pounded as she observed the lone bird streak through the air, then disappear off to the left. *It didn't see me. For now.*

As the world turned away from the sun, the darkness closed in. She almost missed the three ravens as they flew by. While she tracked them, a fourth bird swooped down, then shot past her face. She could hear its wings flap with furious energy as it settled on top of the post behind her head. Its screech echoed over the empty field.

It was calling to its brethren.

A warm dribble of fluid tickled the inside of her thighs as her bladder emptied. If the cawing crow hadn't alerted others to her plight, then the pungent smell of urine would. It was only a matter of time.

Within minutes, three crows approached. She didn't know if they were the same ones from before, but when a half dozen more joined them, she realized it didn't matter. The Rending would feel the same whether by the first bird or the last.

Another gust picked up sweaty locks of her hair and twirled them about. One of the crows darted toward her, but the wind diverted its course. It careened to the right before it could reach her. Its angry cry chilled her blood, raising goosebumps on her skin.

The other birds weren't so easily denied. A flurry of ebony feathers surrounded her. She felt the pinch and scrape of claw and beak. One after another, the crows attacked her naked body. They ripped and tore her flesh as they feasted on it. The contradiction between the soft breeze against her skin, and the searing pain of the attack almost broke her sanity.

As a child, she never could have imagined such a fate. Even the tortures of high school couldn't prepare her for this. As an adult, her mundane routines, predictable chores, and an uninspired imagination molded her into a milquetoast housewife who broke out in hives when the local barista didn't put *two* pumps of vanilla syrup into her latte. When the gods made themselves known, the day they rained fire down from the sky, vaporizing oceans and crumbling mountains, her pathetic life washed away. She witnessed the end of the world as she had come to know it at the hands of an all-powerful, unreachable cabal of supernatural beings.

Three years ago, a growing famine decimated civilization which devolved into ragged walled villages filled with the frightened and desperate remnants of humanity. The weekly sacrifices, an attempt to appease the gods' anger, soon devolved into an excuse to destroy rivals, remove obstacles, or simply relieve boredom when an end to the suffering never came.

Today, she had been judged worthy of such "martyrdom." Shackled and stripped naked, she suffered a humiliating march through town where the people pelted her with clumps of mud and feces. She cried and begged for mercy, but they only laughed as they followed the security detail that dragged her forward. When the procession reached the wide expanse near the forest, someone pushed her down. Striking her head on the hard-packed earth, she lost consciousness. She awoke to the setting sun, securely trussed to the ten-foot pole planted in the ground.

She twisted her head back and forth to avoid the piercing beaks. She strained until her skin bruised, but the bindings held firm. The crows continued their slow, deliberate feast. Perhaps when the moon rose into the star-filled heavens, death would finally come for her.

Her eyes fell on the silhouette of a young man standing among the trees at the edge of the clearing. It was Joshua, her husband, but he wasn't alone. Her best friend, Meg, stepped up behind him, and put her hand on his shoulder. The two shared a smile as they pointed at her, their laughter floating on the wind as it caressed her ravaged flesh. Salty tears stung the fresh wounds on her face. She finally realized the truth behind her predicament.

Furrowing her brow and squeezing her eyes closed, she screamed. She shrieked and howled until her lungs burned. When she finished, the meadow lay quiet. Even her betrayers' amusement had died. Then a soft rustle echoed through the trees as the low brush shook and trembled. In the fading light, she saw something move through the woods.

Just before the crows took her eyes, a large, dark blur burst through the trees. The massive bear fell upon the terrified couple with a great roar. When her world went black, she listened to the cries of the beast's victims mingle with the sounds of splintering bones and ripping tissue. As the birds consumed her flesh inch by inch, a chorus of deep, throaty chuckles rumbled across the sky. And she smiled.

Q

The San Antonio heat made George feel as if his knees would buckle under its oppressive weight. The concrete sidewalk radiated with the same fierceness that threatened to melt him from his boat shoes all the way up to his comb-over. George felt hot, tired, hungry, and homesick for the cool, lakeshore breezes of Chicago.

George and Karen approached a four-story white building on the south side of the city. The Fairview, the oldest hotel in San Antonio, made history in 1986 when the entire structure was moved five blocks from its original location to its present address.

"Apparently, the city board wanted to tear it down," George explained to his wife, "but the historical society raised funds to have it moved."

"The whole building?"

"Yep. And here it sits, just as popular as ever. Plus, it's got this exclusive restaurant in it."

"'Q.' That's a funny name for a restaurant. What's it stand for?"

George shrugged. "Beats me. All I know is that the locals rave about it, and you know that's why Dave booked it. Authenticity."

As he held the door open for Karen, a blast of cold air washed over George. He shivered, despite the one hundred and four degree heat outside. He never could get used to the constant fluxuations in temperatures as he entered and exited any structure here. Once inside, the hostess approached them.

"Good evening. Are you here with the Physics Board, too?"

"How'd you know?"

The hostess looked him up and down, her dark eyes flashing with mischief and something else – desire? George pushed his glasses up on his nose, a nervous habit whenever he was near a beautiful woman. She reached out her hand, and George could already feel his skin tingling.

"This."

The woman pointed at the 2011 Physics conference badge still hanging around George's neck. He laughed, and pushed at his glasses again.

"Ah, right. Of course. Good eye."

She smiled and held out her arm. "Right this way."

George smiled, then turned to his wife to indicate she proceed him. Her right eyebrow arched, and the corner of her mouth lifted in a half-smirk.

George cleared his throat. "What?"

"Smooth, genius," she said before following the hostess.

He hung his head and sighed. Mentally, he chided himself for being such a dork, especially in front of his wife, then moved through the restaurant. All of the tables sat empty, except for the ten-top at the back where his coworkers and their wives had already gathered. The only other patrons were two people sitting at the bar, leaned toward each other in a private conversation.

The vacant tables prickled the hairs on his arms, though George couldn't figure out why. It was the middle of the week, and eight o'clock at night. No reason the restaurant should be bustling with activity. But something about the lack of ambient noises – talking, the clank of silverware against china, servers hurrying in and out of the kitchen – set George's teeth on edge.

When he arrived at the table, all the men were talking about free space impedance, and the wives were henpecking the hostess who, at this point, had returned to the podium at the front of the restaurant. George tuned out both conversations and stared back at her, losing himself in a reverie of fantasy.

A sudden tap on his shoulder made him jump. "Wh-what?"

Karen gave him the arched-eyebrow again. "What do you want to order? You know, for dinner?"

George looked up to see a thin, dark-eyed man standing over him with an order pad. The sneer on the waiter's face told George he'd known exactly whom George was staring at, possibly even the fantasies running through his mind.

"Oh, I, uh–"

"He'll have the fish," Karen told the waiter.

"Very good. I'll be right back with your drinks."

The waiter smirked at George again. He felt his face flush with heat as he looked at Karen. "Thanks. I was totally out of it, I guess."

"Uh, huh. I'm going to the ladies' room."

Karen gave him a warm smile, then walked away

through the restaurant. By the time the waiter served the drinks and appetizers, Karen hadn't returned. George looked at his watch, but since he didn't know what time she'd left, he had no idea how long she'd been gone. He leaned forward to get Laurie's attention, one of the physicists' wives.

"Hey, Laurie? Can you go down to the restroom and see if Karen is still there? She's been gone a while now."

"Really?"

Laurie looked at her watch, then her eyes widened. "Wow, she's been gone for about twenty minutes. I'll go check it out."

"Thanks."

She patted George's hand, then excused herself from the table. None of the others seemed to notice as they scarfed appetizers, and guzzled their drinks. George studied his coworkers and wives. They were all laughing and pushing at each other, slopping their drinks down their shirts or onto the table. Joe and Dave shoveled handfuls of crusted bread soaked in herbed olive oil onto each other's faces, the oil dribbling down their chins, the masticated food rolling around in their open mouths. Robert was building a miniature fort out of the roasted asparagus.

What the hell was wrong with them? Were they drunk already? George could only see one glass in front of each person, so either they were all serious lightweights in the drinking department, or his logical mathematical brain was telling him something was wrong.

George picked up his glass of water and held it under his nose. He couldn't smell anything at first, and almost put the glass down. But instinct told him to sniff again, and when he did, the odor of something antiseptic mixed with campfire smoke stung his nostrils. Something else lay under those odors as well. If he had to guess, he'd say dirt and blood.

While his friends slobbered all over each other, the remaining wives had fallen asleep. Sheila snored in a pile of risotto; Rose had leaned back, her head tilted at what looked like a painful angle over the back of her chair, and smacked her lips between breaths.

George pushed back his chair, and eased himself up. He felt if he didn't disturb this surreal dinner scene, maybe he could escape unharmed.

Escape? Why had that word popped into his head? He didn't know, but every cell in his body told him he had to find Karen, and get out of here before it was too late.

George backed away from the table as slowly as his panicked brain would allow. When he felt he'd reached a safe distance, he turned around. He almost bumped into another table, and as he maneuvered around it, it finally dawned on him why the empty restaurant had so disturbed him. Though no one sat at this table in front of him, a tan sport coat hung on the back of one chair. A folded napkin, smeared with tomato sauce, sat next to a half-eaten serving of lasagna. The smell of a flowery perfume lingered over the full glass of wine with a bright, red lipstick print on its edge.

To George, it looked like who ever had been here simply got up in the middle of their meals, and never returned. He looked around at the other tables: full or half-eaten entrées, tall glasses of water beading condensation onto white tablecloths; sweaters, jackets, purses, wraps, and scarves hung from empty chairs; steaming cups of coffee and tea, aperitifs, melted ice cream, and congealed fondues sat untasted at every table.

Panic surged in his chest again as he thought of Karen. George ran toward the hostess station. The dark-haired beauty sat behind the podium, filing her nails, and looked up at him. The cruel smile on her lips, and the hatred burning in her eyes startled him enough to stop running and stand before her.

She laughed, a deep contemptuous sound. "Is there something wrong, sir?"

"Where's my wife?"

She tapped the file to her lips and batted her eyes. "Your wife? Hmm...I know she was around here somewhere."

Her eyes, no longer brown, but deep black, shifted in the direction of the stairs that led to the restrooms. George ran to them, leaping down two at a time, until he reached an open seating area. The bright red carpet, which had probably been plush and perfect at some point, looked worn and matted. Dark blotchy stains marred the fibers, mostly along the edges at the walls. The overstuffed furniture matched the carpet's dinginess, making the whole room appear haggard.

George scanned the room, and the only marked doors he saw were "Staff Only," "Conference Room," and "Custodian." The floor in front of the janitor's door seemed to have the largest and darkest stains. Combining that with the strange behavior of his colleagues, the missing patrons, as well as the odd demeanor of the hostess, George feared the worst for his wife.

He almost went back upstairs when he noticed a small printed sign"Restroom"with an arrow pointing to the right. Frowning, George looked at the wall, but saw no opening. He took two steps forward, and his change in perspective showed a small narrow corridor. It was as if someone had painted the walls in order to camouflage the hallway. But why?

George moved down the hallway to the only door which lay at the far end. A single word was painted on it: ENTER. As there were no other doors, he assumed it was one of those unisex bathrooms you see in those high-powered lawyer shows on TV. Even if it wasn't, George had to find out if Karen was in there.

Before he could open the door, George heard a soft giggle, and turned to see the hostess standing two feet behind him. He'd never heard her approach, and his heart tripped with fear.

"Where is she? Wh-where's my wife?"

The woman only smiled as her gaze shifted to the door, then back to George.

"You took her, didn't you? Karen, and all the others. Why?"

"Because Qingu commands it."

She reached for the knob and pulled the door open. What looked like a swirling vortex of blood churned just beyond the opening. A raging wind blew out from the center, its roar deafening, almost bringing George to his knees. A long, black tendril of energy snaked out, and wrapped itself around George's body. A flurry of images and sounds enveloped him.

He watched as a bloody, raging battle played out before his eyes. A multitude of gods fought against one another, the image of a beautiful goddess hovering over them. The earth itself formed from their collective corpses; the stars and heavens sparkled into existence along the shining shafts of flung arrows; the beasts of the world stumbled their first steps out of the pools of sweat and tears of the fallen deities.

And the final battle, between Qingu and Marduk,

played out as each god fought for their beautiful queen. As Qingu lay dying and defeated, his blood was taken to create the human race, and his body was sent to the black abyss, to rule over the land of the demons.

"Do you see?" the hostess shouted, bringing George back to the present. "Qingu was betrayed and his blood stolen. We are only returning what is rightfully his!"

As George tried to grab her, the dark energy pulled him into its swirling maw. His screams lasted only a moment before she slammed the door closed. The sudden silence disoriented her for a moment before she shook her head, smoothed her hands over her dark tresses, then made her way back upstairs to the dining room and the remaining sacrifices.

The following afternoon, the hostess stood before the open door. The vortex was gone, but what looked like the flat surface of a blood-filled sea lay in its place. She bowed her head and spoke.

"What do you command, Lord Qingu?"

The deep rumbling timbre of her god's voice washed over her. "Return...my...blood..."

"As you wish."

She closed the door, then leaned on it until she heard the latch snap into place. Making her way upstairs, she called out to one of the waiters.

"Aiemapt, how are the reservations coming?"

"We are only half full tonight, Samira," he answered as he stared down at this shoes.

She backhanded him and he stumbled.

"Would you prefer to be the one to satiate the Lord's desires? If not, I suggest you hustle outside, and drum up some business before you end up on Qingu's table."

The waiter nodded, then scurried away. Samira

smirked. She wasn't worried. Perhaps a thousand years ago they may have lacked a sufficient population. But today, just like in New York, Detroit, Boston, Chicago, and dozens of other cities before this one, she and the other faithful disciples would never want for an ample supply of sacrifices for Lord Qingu.

PSYCHOBABBLE

As Gloria shoveled another spoonful of chocolate ice cream into her mouth, she stared at the business card on the counter. Her friend's words echoed in her head.

"You need to move on, Gloria. Ron took the bank account, the Corvette, and that twenty-year old slut to California. He's not coming back. Get over it."

She parroted her friend's voice in a sing-song lilt, ice cream dribbling down her chin. Gloria wondered if Dr. Girault's specializations of "grieving, depression, and anxiety therapies" might actually help, or just push her deeper into depression. It probably wouldn't hurt to talk to him at least once.

When Gloria approached the one-story red brick building on the day of her appointment, a middle-aged woman exited the front door. Her teased blonde hair had been shellacked into the shape of a cotton ball. Her white blouse was buttoned up to her neck, and her cream-colored pants had been ironed with a crease that looked sharp enough to cut flesh from bone.

Her immaculate appearance wasn't what caught Gloria's eye. It was the whiffle bat the woman held as she swung it back and forth in front of her, as if fending off an invisible attacker. Gloria couldn't discern her mumblings, but her voice sounded gruff and full of hate. The woman got into a white Mazda Miata and drove away, leaving Gloria to stare after her for several minutes.

When she entered the lobby, an assault of bright hues hit Gloria. Reds, yellows, and oranges colored the walls, floors, and even the furniture, like the entire lobby was set aflame. Overwhelmed, she was unable to move forward. A voice to her right snapped her out of her stupor.

"Mrs. Banner?"

Gloria looked over at a young woman behind an oversized desk. She smiled as she approached.

"Yes, I have a ten o'clock with Dr. Girault."

"Please have a seat. We'll call you back in a few minutes."

Gloria frowned. "Don't I have to fill out any paperwork?"

"No."

She offered no further explanation, so Gloria did as instructed. She'd just begun to thumb through the latest trashy magazine when the receptionist called her.

"Mrs. Banner? The doctor will see you now. Please follow Kent."

Gloria looked up to see a tall, well-muscled man standing next to an open door. She smiled at him, but his stoic demeanor never shifted. His chocolate brown eyes regarded her with indifference for three seconds before he turned away, then moved down a narrow hallway.

She quickly followed, scanning the various diplomas and awards dotting the right wall, and a disturbing assortment of art hanging on the left. Flaming buildings and charred corpses; demons tearing apart the damned of Hell; *The Nightmare* by Fuseli. The imp's eyes followed her as she moved ahead.

Kent stopped, and she ran into his back. Gloria mumbled an apology, but he simply opened a door at the end of the hall and motioned her inside. She thanked him, but he had already closed the door against her nose. Gloria stepped back, then turned at the sound of rustling papers. Dr. Girault sat in a gothic style chair, the black leather worn at the armrests. In contrast to the lobby outside, his office stood stark in its spartan color scheme of black and white. Gloria blinked as her eyes adjusted to the change.

"Mrs. Banner, please come in. Sit."

Dr. Girault stood to greet her, holding out a pale, long fingered hand. She shook it, then looked down at the long couch.

"Do I need to lie down?"

"Not yet. Let's get to know each other a bit first. Tell me why you've come."

Gloria sat, her back rigid, not knowing where to begin. As she contemplated her issues, she realized how bitter and pathetic they seemed. Her eyes welled, and she stumbled over her words.

"A few months ago, my husband..."

She found herself unable to continue as the tears spilled and she shook with sobs. Dr. Girault leaned over, and patted her hand.

"He cheated on you? Left you for some tramp?"

Gloria twitched at his blunt tone. She nodded, and he continued.

"I've seen this a hundred times, Mrs. Banner. May I call

you Gloria, since you don't deserve to be shackled to that name anymore?"

"Please."

"Gloria, I know I can sit here and spew all the usual platitudes: you don't deserve this, he's an asshole, don't wallow. But sometimes we need to sit and stew in the miserableness of it all before we can begin to heal. People treat relationship troubles as something not worthy of grieving. They think just because no one died, then there is no "real" loss. Well, I call bullshit."

Gloria looked up at him, and barked out a short laugh.

The doctor smiled. "So, you agree with me. That's good. Very good."

He stood and paced the small office.

"You see, Gloria, I subscribe to what has been called "extreme" therapy. I believe a patient needs to sit with their suffering, really look it in the eye and get comfortable with it, before they can move on. Do you think you can do that?"

Gloria nodded. "My friend keeps telling me to get over it, but I don't feel ready."

"Then stay in the sorrow, Gloria. Bathe in this depression until it floods every cell of your body, every aspect of your soul. Here are some exercises you can do."

By the end of that first week, Gloria felt so much better. She was morose all the time, but didn't mind anymore. She was happy in her sadness, taking pleasure in moping and staring off into space as she dreamed of the life she'd once had. She even felt a small thrill as she held a serrated steak knife to her own throat while staring at herself in the mirror.

Within a few weeks, however, she'd lost the joy of wallowing, and only felt misery again. When she discussed this with Dr. Girault, he smiled.

"I believe that you are ready for the next phase."

"What's that?"

"Gloria, have you ever heard the term, *schadenfreude*?"

She shook her head and he continued.

"*Schadenfreude* is a fantastic German word that means 'to find enjoyment at another's suffering.'"

"You mean how I might find it funny to see my cranky old neighbor trip and fall in her driveway, twisting her ankle?"

"Exactly! When we can find misfortune in others' lives, we often forget the pain in our own."

"But things like that don't happen every day."

"You'd be surprised, Gloria. And if you don't see any misery, you can always create some."

"What do you mean?"

Dr. Girault didn't elaborate. He ended the session and bid her good day. Sitting at a red light, a young man crossed through the walkway in front of Gloria's car, burdened with several heavy boxes marked "fragile." Imagining how easy it would be to trip him up, she laughed aloud. Then she understood what Dr. Girault meant. Glancing around for nearby onlookers, Gloria leaned on the horn. Startled, the guy jumped, and dropped every box. Even through the closed windows, Gloria heard a great crash as the breakables shattered around him.

When the light turned green, she veered to the right to drive around the distressed fellow. This was going to be fun.

Over the coming weeks she shared her exploits with Dr. Girault. He praised her creativity, dedication, and perseverance. After six months, he introduced the next stage.

"You've done very well so far, but it's time for Phase Three. For some, it's the last stage in their grieving. For others..."

He trailed off, leaving her to wonder what could be in store for her future.

"Phase Three is to move you past all the afflictions, yours and outsiders. Even if you no longer suffer, the distress of others hurts us all. So, I want you to end the pain, Gloria."

"What do you mean–"

"End it."

He stared at her over his notepad, his eyebrows arched high. She didn't understand but nodded anyway.

"Good. Same time next week, then?"

"Yes. Good bye, Doctor."

She drove the long way home, pondering today's session. Was she just supposed to end her exploits, or did he mean something else?

As she slowed to a stop at a red light, a homeless man lunged at her car, and began cleaning her windshield with a dirty rag. He smiled at her around a lone, blackened stump of a tooth.

"Clean your car, lady?"

She started to say no, but stopped. She stared at the man's raggedy appearance, the desperation in his smile, and the hopelessness in his eyes.

"End it."

Dr. Girault's message became clear in that moment. She opened her window and smiled.

"I hope you don't think I'm being condescending, but how would you like to earn some money?"

An hour later, Gloria stood over the dismembered corpse of Harold, the homeless man with no job, no money, no prospects. A faceless number in a crowd of the invisible whose absence would never be felt. This poor man wouldn't have to suffer the elements or know hunger ever again.

Gloria's exuberance quickened her blood. Listening to his screams excited her in a way she'd never known. She hoped Dr. Girault would be proud.

Edward Girault smiled from his prone position on the therapist's couch. Dr. Reynolds buried his nose in his scribbled notes, mumbling banalities as he always did during Edward's sessions.

"I do think I'm improving, Dr. Reynolds. In the past, people like my newest patient would have caused me to falter. However, she's improving steadily with accepted therapies," Edward lied.

"That's wonderful," Dr. Reynolds replied.

"I do admit that it hasn't been easy, but I see now how my extreme therapy practices were just an excuse to fuel my Conduct Disorder."

"Good, good."

More notes and murmuring. Edward knew from his first session that Dr. Reynolds would be the perfect therapist. The state review board ordered that Edward get help, and only from what it considered a qualified specialist, if he wanted to continue practicing psychology, at least. Edward had no intention of informing the board that seventy-eight-year old Dr. Reynolds was more interested in ogling his secretary than helping people.

Edward babbled what could be deemed as valuable progress for each recorded session that the review board received an hour later. All the while, he would continue to manipulate his own patients, even helping some cover up crimes, to make them believe his therapies were working.

At the end of the hour, Edward sat up. "So, what do you think, doc?"

"I think you've made excellent progress, Dr. Girault. I even feel I can recommend to the board that this be our final appointment."

"That's great news!"

"It's not official, so until you hear differently, plan to return at your regular time next week."

"Of course. Thank you, Dr. Reynolds."

"Think nothing of it. Good-bye."

Edward felt his lip curl into a sneer as he left the office, and walked to his car. "I never do, doc. I never do."

As he drove to his own office, Edward rolled down the window, breathing in the fresh air of the sunny morning. When he entered the lobby, he smiled at the receptionist.

"Good morning, Miss Wright. Any messages?"

"Just one from Gloria Banner. She was hoping to come in early today. She's eager to speak to you about something that happened over the weekend."

Miss Wright gave Dr. Girault a sly smile, and he squeezed her hand after she passed him the note.

"Please tell Gloria she may come in at her earliest convenience."

As Miss Wright dialed the phone, Dr. Girault whistled on the way to his office.

CLOUD

He waved his hand through the vapor around his head. "Knock it off."

The cloud dissipated but soon returned. He cut at it with a magazine. "I said, stop."

It remained clear for a minute, but the mist swirled again. Throwing the magazine down, he stood.

"Dammit, Michael, this is the last time. You are grounded. No blood for a week!"

The vapor solidified into a young boy, who folded his arms across his chest, and glared at his father.

"And put those fangs back in or it's two weeks."

The boy retracted his teeth, and stomped away in anger.

WHY BE NORMAL?

The swings creaked as each child pumped out his little legs to soar higher and higher into the sky. The slide flexed as a little boy whizzed down on his backside, his slight weight just enough pressure to cause the thin metal to buckle under his passing. Mothers and nannies sat on benches watching over their brood, or looking at each other intently. A small giggle or quiet laugh could be heard from time to time, but there was no talking. No one moved his or her mouth at all except to breathe or eat.

This isn't a playground for the deaf or mute. This is a telepathic society. Everyone is capable of communicating with the mind instead of the mouth; the ability to move and affect objects or people with just a thought, otherwise known as telekinesis, is the norm. There are many variations on this theme, but they all boil down to the same thing – everyone can do it. Well, maybe not everyone.

I, Jason Lattan, am a freak. I am a weirdo, a loser, different, the devil, possessed by the devil, the devil's spawn, special, one-dimensional, a half-brainer, handicapped. I can't talk to others with my mind. I can't move my coffee cup from one side of the kitchen table to the other with just a thought. I can't let my mom know I'm coming for dinner without picking up the phone.

Of course, it costs about $800.00 to buy a phone these days. Any kind of "special" equipment is expensive – phones, computers, typewriters, microphones – anything that deals with verbal or written communication. There's a special line at Buzz's Burgers for those who have to use the vulgar speech. I'm the only one who's ever in it. Even construction equipment is being phased out. Why would anyone pay half a million dollars for a crane when one or two people can do the same work for a lot less?

POP!

I've always tried to imagine what life would be like if more people spoke. All the different sounds of voices – whiny, nasal, gruff, weak, strong, loud, soft – would combine to make a beautiful symphony. Crying, yelling, shouting, whispering. All would be welcome in my world. But it's hard to play in an orchestra when you're the only one with an instrument. To be honest, though, I'm not the only one who isn't telepathic or tele-anything else.

Growing up, I attended a special school for others like me. We all rode together on a special bus, a bright blue vehicle with whitewall tires. Of course, we were laughed at and teased. We were the objects of cruelty and hate, scorn and malice. And the practical jokes? There was no way for us to fight back. How exactly do you stop someone from pulling your pants down when they're standing ten feet away?

The bigotry didn't exactly improve with age. There are always people, grown men and women, who are afraid of the different, of what they don't understand. So, as is human nature, they automatically hate what they fear, and try to destroy it. Not right out. Not immediately. It's usually a slow torture of stares, covert glances, whispered criticisms, not-so-subtle pointing, laughing, and other emotional timebombs, set strategically over the years that eventually run down their clocks and explode. Many people like me, the "handicapped," can't take it. They usually have a nervous breakdown by the time they reach thirty, and are carted off to some sewer of an institution, more fit for housing garbage than humans.

Sometimes they go on a bloody rampage, taking out as many of the Teles as possible. At least they *attempt* to rampage. As soon as a Tele sees what's happening, he'll mentally restrain the gimp until the cops arrive, then they cart him off to the sewer. I never used to condone this kind of behavior, but now I can understand what drives some of us to do it.

I used to work at the public library in town. It had a special area for the handicapped, and I managed it. The head librarian, Ms. Marla Thompson, put up with me because she had to. I knew she hated being around the handicapped. Not because she told me. She'd never stoop so low as to actually speak to anyone, let alone a gimp. When she rolled a book cart behind me as I was standing on a chair trying to reach one of the upper shelves, and I turned to step down and almost broke my neck after tumbling over the cart, I got the general idea.

POP! POP!

I quit that afternoon. I know that just gave her what she wanted, but there was nothing else I could do. She could have ended any retaliation I planned before it got started. But shortly after I left, I started to run an experiment. I tried to plan something out, and actually execute it to its full completion, before anyone stopped me. Nothing big at first. Little things, like dropping water balloons on people from the fifth floor of the First National building, or throwing rocks against people's windows in the middle of the night. Both of those adventures landed me a couple of nights in jail, but it was worth it. I was beginning to learn the Tele's limits. They may have all these great powers, but we can throw a few monkey wrenches into their works from time to time. Keeps them on their toes.

I started these tests a couple of years ago. You may think it was Ms. Thompson that drove me to it, but that's not really true. Granted, she was a small-minded, miserable, old bitch, but the catalyst for my new hobby was an old friend of mine. Davey Archer and I went to the same school and were in all the same "special" classes. We only lived a block apart, so naturally we became great friends. I lost track of him after high school, though I saw a newspaper article two years ago about one of the special people who went berserk and tried to shoot up a bunch of Teles at the local mall. As I read on, the story mentioned the shooter by name – David Archer.

The article went on to explain his family background, his handicapped status, the history of low paying, scum jobs, and being an all-around slacker and burden to society. He'd managed to shoot two Teles, killing one, before being captured and shipped off to the Anderson Psychiatric Hospital. The APH, if I remember correctly, is one of the worst hospitals – and I use that term very loosely – in the entire country. The locals call it the All-mighty Piss Hole. The inmate population is about 220, and the staff to patient ratio is one to thirty. There are only seven doctors in the whole place on rotating shifts, so there are only three doctors in the hospital on active duty at all times.

When I found out Davey was in there, I made plans to visit him. The patients in places like that were usually ninety-percent handicapped, so there was always someone on duty who would answer the phone and talk. When I called, the nurse told me he'd had no visitors since checking in, so she was thrilled to hear from me. When I inquired about his family, she hesitated and changed the subject. Davey had been the family's dirty little skeleton and now they had a nice large stinking closet, paid for by the state, in which to safely, and quietly, tuck him away.

POW!

I'd heard all the horror stories about the hospital, but nothing could have prepared me for what I saw that day. I pulled up in the front semi-circle drive, and parked my car in front of the door. I stood staring up at this hunk of dirty grey concrete known as APH. It was ten stories high, and the concrete was cracked and broken off in many places. Brown rusty water had leaked down the sides from the old battered eaves and drain spouts. It looked as if the building was an enormous alien creature that had been stabbed in the head, and the blood dripped down its body, finally clotting and drying on its limbs.

It was as if they didn't even keep up the façade of being a decent care facility, let alone make you think that humans, or any life form, were being cared for in this godforsaken hole. About one-third of the windows were cracked or broken out completely. The grounds surrounding the building were shoddy at best. Half of the grass was alive, and the rest was brown and dead, or yellowed and dying.

I approached the two front, glass doors, and saw an orderly wiping them down. As I got closer, I noticed the man was merely smearing greasy water in lazy circles with a dark, filthy rag, not really cleaning anything. He was just going through the motions, as if trying to avoid other, more strenuous work by looking busy.

The nurse I spoke to on the phone was at the check-in desk. She was a petite woman with flat, yellow hair, and Coke-bottle glasses. She smiled at me, saying how happy she was that David would finally have a visitor. I suddenly felt like punching her in the face, smashing her thick glasses into her eyeballs, and stabbing her in the heart with the sign-in pen. But she was handicapped, like me. Just like Davey. So, I swallowed my violent urges, and simply returned her smile.

She directed me to the sixth floor, room 620, all the way down on the left. She commented on how David was so lucky to have his own cell. They were forty patients over the building's capacity, and some had to share cells. That's what she called them. Not rooms, but cells. As she processed the paperwork, and got my Visitor badge ready, I looked around. The walls, at one point, must have been a cheery yellow, and the floor white linoleum tile. Now the walls were faded and dirty, the paint chipped and peeling. The tile was the same color as the concrete face of the building. Most of them were buckled and cracked, and several tiles were missing all together, leaving brown-black spots scattered down the hallway that looked like scabs.

I took my badge from the duty nurse, and headed for the elevators. As soon as the doors opened on the sixth floor, the first thing I noticed was the smell. Now, I've been in some of the filthiest men's rooms in the city, but this was putrid. I had to hold my coat sleeve over my mouth, though the stench still clogged my throat, making me gag. I wasn't sure I'd make it down the hall before puking. There was another orderly sitting at a desk next to the elevator, and to this day, I still don't know how he could sit there without some kind of mask over his face. Maybe after a few years – hell, maybe only months – all sense of smell is burned out of your nose from the exposure.

He barely looked up at me as I showed him my badge and announced who I wanted to visit. He waved in the general direction of Davey's room. His curled lip indicated disgust and annoyance at having his afternoon nap interrupted. Before I could even ask, he plucked the question from my mind and answered it.

"Last door on the left and yes, you are the first person to visit him. Ever. Poor bastard just sits in there all day, humming or mumbling to himself."

I opened my mouth for the second question, but he beat me to it again.

"Nope. Never goes outside either."

I smirked in his general direction, then walked down the hall to Davey's room. I mean, cell. The walls were a sickly green, like rotting flesh. I noticed the once white tiles, directly surrounding each doorway, were stained urine yellow as if each inmate, well, urinated on the floor of their cells. Eventually it seeped under the door, soaking into the porous tile. Didn't they give these people access to toilets?

A voice echoed down the hall to me, "Yeah but they don't use them."

"Will you knock it off?" I shouted back to the orderly.

I approached Room 620, the urine stain on the floor matching all the others. Grimacing, I looked through the eight-by-ten-inch window, cut into the middle of the door, two feet down from the top. In place of glass, there were two-inch thick bars spaced one inch apart, making it difficult for the inmates to reach out and grab anyone passing by.

The cell sat in gauzy shadow. The small, square patch

of light I could see came from the hallway. When I put my head up to the small window, most of that square disappeared behind my shadow. There was a window high in the opposite wall, about nine feet up, and out of reach of the inmates, even if they stood on their beds. The grey afternoon offered some dingy, natural light, but I could imagine what the cell must feel like at night. The small patch of wan, yellow light spilling in from the hallway, like a little window in your coffin, allowing you to see just the head of the shovel as it pours dirt over you, and your final resting place.

The corners of the cell were obscured in darkness, and I couldn't see Davey anywhere. Just as I was about to yell for the orderly, one of the grey smudges in the back corner moved. It crept along the far wall, inch by inch. An arm, caked in filth, reached up, and scrabbled its fingers at the padded surface next to what I could only assume to be Davey's face. My horrified intake of breath caught Davey's attention. He turned to look at me.

His once chocolate brown hair was white. Whatever wasn't matted down with dirt was sticking out or up, like a cartoon character who had just grabbed a live, electric wire. His hospital gown was stiff with stains and filth, as if made of cardboard. His feet were bare, and I could see a raw band of flesh on each ankle, indicating that the staff shackled him often, more likely from boredom than any need to immobilize a violent attack. The person I was staring at was no more capable of harming anyone than a slug on Prozac.

I raised my hand to the window, clamping one of the bars in a white-knuckled grip, and whispered his name. "Davey."

His gaze darted back and forth, unfocused. He didn't recognize me. Turning away to look at the wall, Davey scratched and picked at it. He began humming, an old song we used to sing together in school. When I recognized it, I started to cry. Tears spilled down my cheeks, and I could do nothing to stop them. Back when we were young, whenever one of us gimps was thrown into the APH, Davey and I would buy a case of beer, get slobbering drunk, and sing "Hotel California" by The Eagles until we were hoarse. I sang as he hummed.

When I got to the chorus, I was barely whispering the words, and I realized Davey wasn't humming anymore. He was looking at me. I mean, really looking *at* me. He stood slowly, his balled fists pressed against his mouth, his eyes wide in surprise and recognition. Shuffling towards me, his eyes never left mine. I grasped the bars with both hands in anticipation. He reached tentatively, gently for my hands. He had to stand on his tiptoes to be at eye level with me. His blue eyes were flat, almost colorless, but there was awareness swimming in their depths.

As I finished the chorus, he opened his mouth to speak, baring teeth that were yellow and blackened with rot. His jaw trembled as his lips formed the first words he'd spoken in years. My name rattled across his vocal chords.

"Jason?"

I wept my affirmative because I couldn't speak. As awful as this place was, and as horrified as I was at Davey's life now, I was thrilled he knew me. I pressed my face against the bars and let him trace my features with his fingers. We were both crying and laughing, snot bubbling out our noses, and spit dribbling down our chins.

But my laughter quickly subsided as Davey's escalated into a cackle of hysteria. He pulled at his hair, and clawed at his face. His screams echoed down the hall, but none of the other inmates joined in. They all knew this moment was for

Davey, and him alone. I shouted his name, but I could barely hear myself over the din. Suddenly, he quieted. He stood motionless in the middle of the cell, his arms slack at his sides.

He looked up at me, smiled softly, then whispered, "Thank you, Jason."

He dropped to the floor, like a two-ton weight had fallen on top of him. His legs just buckled, and down he went. I called to him.

"Davey? *DAVEY!*"

He was dead. I stood there, watching him for fifteen minutes, and he never moved. His eyes stared off at a spot just above and to the left of me, and his mouth curled in a sweet smile. I turned to look down the hall, and the orderly was still sitting calmly at his desk. My mind went dark. Rage threw a shadow over all my thoughts as I walked towards him. He looked up at me as I approached, a frown creasing his brow. He had no idea what I was thinking or planning because, consciously, I didn't know myself. Only after I had pulled him from his chair, and broken his neck, did I realize what I had wanted to do all along.

Staring down at his prone body, it was my turn to frown. I had wanted to kill him. I wanted it so badly that I not only tasted it, I was choking on it. But the whole time I walked toward him, I thought of Davey. I wanted to kill this man for Davey. For the hell these people had put him through the last years of this life. For the hell they'd put *all* of us through.

CRACK!

That's when I started running my experiments. If I practiced enough discipline, I could disguise or block my thoughts from the Teles before they discovered what I was planning. After about a year, I increased my efforts to include activities such as shoving a Tele down the subway steps, or pushing one in front of a speeding car. But I learned the closer you got to them, the harder it was to run away, once the deed was done. All the other Teles in the vicinity who witnessed my deeds would all pitch in to restrain me for the cops.

So, I had to work on my long-distance guerrilla warfare. Throwing a grenade into a crowded, public square was my first success at anonymous fighting tactics. After lobbing the pesky little explosive into the crowd, I just kept on walking. Once the explosion rocked the square, I turned around like everyone else, pretending to be shocked and horrified. Unfortunately, I only killed one person, and injured three. Luckily, they were all Teles, but that's when I realized I could have hurt handicappers, my brethren, if you will.

I needed to come up with a more selective killing process. And that's when it hit me—guns. Guns were very impersonal, great for long-distance, and could be concealed relatively easily within the folds of a full-length coat, or bulky jacket. And for the most part, it only takes a small movement, a flick of my wrist, to bring it up and squeeze off a shot.

I did my research and my field work and found that an H&K USP, equipped with suppressor, was perfect. I could walk through a crowded shopping mall, or even a partially deserted parking lot, and take down anyone within forty feet, and still not be suspected. You may be wondering how I can tell a Tele from a gimp just by looking at them, am I right? Well, believe me. Growing up gimp gives you all the clues you need. But, just to be safe, I always try and take out Teles that are in a group, or at least a pair.

You see, when two or more Teles get together, they never speak verbally, only telepathically. It makes them feel superior. They may gesture, or jump up and down to make a point, but they never open their mouths. It's a simple matter to pick them out of a crowd. Besides, for every gimp there are about 500,000 Teles, so I'm pretty safe.

CRRRAAAACK!!

Shit. Suppressor's wearing out on me. I've got to go find a safe place to put on the new one. That's the only bad part. These damn silencers wear out after just a handful of shots, but I got 'em all today. Didn't miss a single one. Thinking about Davey really helped. Maybe I should tell you about the time that I ran into Davey's mom, after I visited him at the APH. Nah. I'd better think happy thoughts until I can get this suppressor replaced. Wouldn't want to give myself away now would I?

CROOKED

Screeeeeeeee!

David stopped the car, and tilted his head. "Did you hear that?"

Marilyn rolled her eyes. "There's nothing wrong with the car, David."

"You're telling me you didn't hear that?"

"Are you going to do this the whole way? We won't get there until next week."

He glared at her, but released the brake and continued forward. The winding mountain road would give him plenty more chances to listen. If the damn brake pads were worn out already, he was gonna sue that damn brake shop.

As the car approached another bend, he lifted his foot off of the gas pedal, then gently pressed the brake.

Screeeeeeeeee!

He slammed his foot to the floor. The screech sounded like it came from above the car, not below it. Marilyn's seatbelt locked as she was thrown forward.

"God dammit, David! What the hell are you doing?"

He thought he heard a thump on the roof when the car

jerked to a stop. Marilyn glanced up for a brief second, and he saw it.

"You did hear it, didn't you?" he asked.

"I didn't hear anything. Can we please just go?"

David heard the tremble in her voice. He stared at her for a moment longer, then eased the car forward again.

They drove for several minutes before another curve forced him to slow down. But before he ever touched the brake, the eerie shriek sounded again. This time, Marilyn gripped his arm.

"Don't stop, David. Just keep going."

The car swerved through the arc, then he accelerated. Another turn approached, but he didn't reduce their speed. The screech came louder than the squeal of tires. There was definitely something on the roof.

Another great scream echoed around them when a blackened claw punctured the roof of the car. Marilyn screamed, and David wrestled with the wheel as the car careened through another curve. Several more claws punched through, and pulled away a large portion of the panel. David dared a glance upward, and caught the grim visage of a hideous creature – mottled, lumpy skin, clear viscous fluid dripping from jagged fangs, and one glowing, orange eye that stared down at him.

"Jesus, Mary, and Joseph."

"What – "

"Marilyn, don't look. Just hold on."

Ahead, David spied a yellow sign adorned with a black, snake-like picture. Maybe they could throw the creature off as they drove through one of those turns. He jammed the accelerator to the floor just as the creature stabbed another hole in the roof.

Marilyn screamed – from the monster or the hairpin

turn, he couldn't be sure. David whipped the car through the first bend, and the creature rolled to the side, but maintained its hold. As he hugged the next turn, it rolled the other way, still not relinquishing its grasp.

Marilyn continued screaming as the creature continued tearing the roof apart. David spotted the next sign, the last one before the road stretched out straight for two miles, prior to the highway: "Sharp Turn Ahead, 35MPH."

This was his last chance to cast the creature off. If he failed...

He mashed the accelerator down, and rocketed toward the final curve. Marilyn had stopped screaming, and placed her hand over his on the wheel. They gave each other one last look and smile, each mouthing "I love you," right before he pulled the wheel sharply to the left.

For what felt like several minutes, but were merely seconds, the squealing tires and screeching beast sung a terrible harmony as the car threatened to roll. It lifted on the left side, and David thought they were finished. But with one final scream, the creature finally let go, and tumbled off into the scrubby landscape.

The car leveled, and they hit the straightaway at 55 mph. David accelerated to seventy-five, putting as much distance between them and what almost became their last day on earth. He and Marilyn shared nervous laughter as they drove on, but they soon quieted as he wondered if the next car would be so lucky.

DIVIDED

"It's mine!"

"I saw it first."

"Give it."

"*You* give it."

"The oldest of the Sigbin family gets dibs, and that's me!"

"Finders keepers, and I'm the one who found it."

The tug of war between the two brothers ended with a great shriek and a violent, wet tearing of flesh. The two beasts looked down as a small pile of bloody innards plopped onto the dusty path. Each held one half of the infant's corpse.

"Oh, great. Look what you did. Now, we have to get a whole new one."

"Me? You're the one who wouldn't let go. And you should have, because it was mine."

"Are you joking? It was mine, and you know it."

The siblings continued arguing as they trudged through the jungle, returning to the nearby village for another snack.

HR

Paul pulled into the parking garage, his sour stomach and clenched jaw giving him a headache. He'd pretty much felt this way for the past three months. He'd taken a lateral move within the company, which he hoped would boost his career in the right direction. After the first couple of weeks, Paul realized that the client would always be the client (read: jerk-offs,) and he couldn't do a damn thing about it. He had so many great ideas to move them forward into the new year, but they would have nothing to do with it. They liked things to be the way they've always been – traditional, inside the norm, not too innovative, and cheap. In other words, the same boring shit the company had done for the past forty years.

Paul shuffled from his car to the lobby of his building. He stood slump-shouldered in the elevator and, after getting off at the fourth floor, lumbered over to his office. He closed the door, locked it, and sat down behind his desk. Leaning forward on his elbows, he covered his face with his hands. He stayed that way for half an hour, mentally going over where he'd made all the wrong choices in his career.

He loved advertising, and he was good at it. For twenty years, he'd worked for this company and gave them everything he had. He saw his coworkers more than he saw his own family, which was why he got divorced. Luckily, he and Marsha never had any kids, so there was no guilt for screwing up any additional lives and feeling responsible when they took to the rooftops with submachine guns. He'd put in ten-, thirteen-, sometimes seventeen-hour days for this job, but he received no encouragement – neither from the client nor his supervisor, Doug. Doug only supported the client, and if they wanted to ostracize Paul, then Doug was with them all the way.

The only good thing about his supervisor was Doug's assistant, Jill. Jill was a pretty, young woman of twenty-five, fifteen year's Paul's junior, with long, blonde hair and shining, blue eyes. She'd felt bad about the way they treated Paul because she shared in his enthusiasm and his fresh ideas. But that wasn't the only thing she shared with him. She and Paul had been secretly dating for eight months. Not that they were embarrassed about their age difference. It was hard enough to have a relationship these days without the entire company getting involved.

A soft knock at the door broke his reverie. "Come on in."

Jill peeked through the open doorway. "Are you in the middle of something? I just needed to drop off the budget report from Doug."

Paul grimaced at his supervisor's name, but motioned for Jill to enter. She held a manila folder in her hands, but it appeared empty. He frowned in confusion, looking from the folder to her face.

She blushed a soft pink, and sat down across from him, whispering. "I don't actually have a report from Doug. I said that in case anyone was listening. I just really wanted to come see you."

Paul relaxed with a smile. He held up a finger, then quickly walked to his door. Seeing no one out in the hall, he eased the door closed, then locked it. As he turned, he almost knocked Jill over, not realizing she had snuck up behind him. She giggled and wrapped her arms around his waist. She was a petite woman, and only came up to his collarbone, so he rested his chin on her head and enveloped her in his arms. He sighed, swaying with her in his arms, for several minutes. With her face pressed against his chest, he couldn't hear her muffled question and sadly, pulled back and asked her to repeat it.

"I asked if you were all right. You've been very down lately."

"I'm fine. Just frustrated. Between you and me, I don't think I'm long for this company."

She nodded her head. "I figured as much. I'm just worried that if you go, you won't keep in touch. Seems like everyone who leaves this company forgets all about us, like they dropped of the face of the earth."

He cupped her head in his hands. "No matter what happens with this job, I will definitely keep in touch with you, all right?"

She smiled, then quickly backed up. "Oh, I almost forgot. Did you hear about Brian? They fired him. Can you believe it?"

Brian Rollins worked in the same department and was one of Paul's closest friends. Brian knew about Paul and Jill, but had the decency to keep it to himself. Paul's mood darkened further with this news. Brian was the only advocate of his new ideas. With him gone, it was only a matter of time before the company gave Paul the boot.

"What the hell's going on in this firm?" Paul asked. "When did this happen? Why didn't he say anything?"

Jill shook her head.

"As far as I know, it was news to him, too. He had a meeting with Doug this morning, and Brian was furious when he left. He said he was told his performance was lacking and to go up to Human Resources for his exit interview immediately, and was expected to leave directly afterward. They even sent someone down from HR to escort him upstairs. That was twenty minutes ago."

"And you haven't seen him come back down yet?"

"Nope."

He kissed her on her forehead. "Thanks. I'm going to go walk over to his office and see what's up. I'll talk to you later."

She squeezed his hand, and left the office first. He turned left down the hall, then around the first corner to Brian's door. It was slightly ajar, and he could see someone moving around inside. Just before he pushed the door open, he noticed it wasn't Brian but Jeff Levon from HR. Jeff was opening drawers and pulling out files, rummaging through all of Brian's things, as if searching for something. Frowning, Paul watched him.

Jeff was becoming increasingly agitated, throwing papers onto the floor, and blowing air through clenched teeth. He sounded like a bull about to charge a matador. Jeff finally stood behind Brian's desk, hands on his hips, and muttered something about a bluff. Paul quickly ducked into the cubicle outside Brian's office just as Jeff stormed out. Fortunately, he turned away from the cube, and walked briskly up the hall toward the elevators.

Paul peeked around the corner. When he could no longer see Jeff, he pushed open the door to Brian's office.

The place was a disaster. Brian would be furious when he got back from his exit interview. He stepped around the mess to stand behind the desk. He wondered what Jeff was looking for. As he turned around, he looked at the bookcase behind him. Most of the binders and booklets had been pulled down, and now laid open on the floor. He bent down and picked up a couple, turning them over in his hands. He looked back up at the bookcase, and saw a small brown envelope taped to the underside of the third shelf.

Frowning, Paul reached up and plucked the envelope free. He studied it, trying to puzzle out its importance. He quickly looked over his shoulder, feeling like he was being watched. After ducking out of Brian's office, Paul returned to his own and locked himself inside. He sat down at his desk, and stared at the envelope. Could this be what Jeff wanted? He flipped it over and tore the flap open. Inside were a flash drive and a short hand-written note. To his surprise, Paul found the note addressed to him.

Paul,

Well, buddy, if you're reading this, it means I've been fired, and I'm already gone. I'm sorry I didn't get a chance to say goodbye. Read what's on the drive and you'll understand. Take care of yourself, and Jill, too. Get out while you still can.

Brian

Paul scratched his head in confusion. He knew Brian clashed with Doug and the client a few times, but he never thought they'd fire him. Why did he leave without coming to say goodbye? And get out of what, the relationship with

Jill? But then why would he tell him to take care of her? Did he mean get out of this job, to quit? He didn't understand what the hell was going on.

Frowning – seemed he did a lot of that lately – Paul picked up the drive and studied it. He swiveled around in his chair and plugged it into his computer. He pulled up its contents and found only one item there: *hr.doc*. He double clicked on it, the screen flashed once, then a ninety-page document opened. It was a table with four columns, starting with the year 1934: Name, Start Date, Exit Date, Confirm Removal. The last column had no information until 1955, the same year the company retained the business of who had become their largest, and only, client. From that point on, the last column was filled with checkmarks, and each former employee appeared to have one.

Confirm Removal? Did they actually check off the dates when Security escorted someone out? He scanned over the names on the list, about twenty per page, and recognized about fifty of them. The tables were marked with a year, beginning with 2018 on the first page, all the way back to the company's beginning on the last. Each person on this list was someone who had been fired or quit, including Brian. But there was no checkmark next to his name. Paul noted the Exit Date for Brian was last Monday. Those bastards in HR knew he was being fired a week ago, and they only told him today.

Paul thought about overhearing Jeff say something about a bluff while searching Brian's office. Did Brian approach them with this information, to blackmail HR into letting him keep his job? From what Paul could see, there was nothing useful that could be used to blackmail anyone. He scanned the list again. This time he noticed a star next to several names, Paul's included. He tried to remember their faces: Cal James, Robin Finny, Sally Johnson, Rick Porter, JC Robbins.

He remembered Rick's last day. The guy was shaking like a leaf as he was escorted up to HR for his exit interview. He looked defeated, but Paul had chalked it up to being fired. Sally had been the same, but she'd quit, so the stars couldn't indicate how or why someone left the company. Cal had made a huge stink. He was shouting and shaking his fists, running around the office, screaming, "Don't let them do this!" Two security guards had been sent up to restrain him and, Paul assumed, escort him from the building.

At the time he had thought it was really sad how Cal was carrying on and on. Thinking back, though, Cal wasn't just distraught at losing his job – he seemed terrified. But of what? Paul looked back to the list, and a few more names jumped out at him, all of them with really odd or extreme reactions to being fired. There was a star next to Brian's name, too. The gears of his brain were almost audibly clicking as he pieced it all together. Each person on this list was either fired or quit; the ones with stars next to their names were the people who were terrified or extremely agitated when they left for HR; and all of those people's fire dates were a week before they worked their last day.

Were they all just freaked out at leaving, or did they all know something? Did they have the same information Brian had copied on this drive, and tried to use it against the company to keep their jobs? Paul was still missing a piece of the puzzle, some other bit of information these people had that terrified them. He needed to find it. And he thought he knew exactly where to find it.

At 5:30, there was a knock at Paul's door. Doug popped his head in, grinning.

"I didn't think I'd see you here this late, Paul."

Paul smiled weakly at him. "Well, I've got to work on this 'Company Goals' document for the client, and it's taking me longer than I anticipated. I probably won't get out of here for another couple of hours. Why are you still here?"

Doug sniffed at the implied insult. "I'm always here until about 6:30, but I've got to get home to the little wifey. Anniversary dinner."

Paul nodded, then looked back down at the document he was working on. Waving absently at his boss, he mumbled, "Well, don't let me keep you. Have a good night."

Doug stood there, surprised at Paul's aloofness. Just as he was about to turn away, Paul looked up at him and caught his expression.

He smiled sheepishly. "Sorry I'm being so blah about your anniversary. Normally I'd say congratulations or something, but I'm just upset about Brian Rollins."

Doug's eyes widened in surprise. "What about Brian?"

Paul frowned. "You fired him this morning, remember?"

Doug sighed, almost with relief, Paul thought. "Oh, yes. Well, that couldn't be helped. He'd been slacking for months now, and fighting with the client constantly. You know how much they hate to argue, Paul."

The last comment was a dig about Paul's recent bouts with the client. Was he next to be fired? He smirked at Doug. "Yeah, I suppose I do. Well, have a happy anniversary. Enjoy dinner."

He looked back down at his work as Doug huffed loudly and walked off. Paul peeked at Doug's stiff back, and chuckled to himself. Once he was alone again, Paul removed Brian's drive from his computer, and put it back in the brown envelope, along with the original note. After locking it in his top drawer, he moved to his office door and listened. He heard one keyboard clacking away, and another person chatting on the phone. Other than that, the only other people around were two maintenance men, emptying wastebaskets and wiping down workstations.

Paul grabbed an empty file folder from his desk drawer, and walked to the elevators. He'd never tried to spy on anyone before, so he hoped the folder added an innocuous manner of purpose. He took the elevator to the eighteenth floor. HR was the only department on this floor, and the quiet indicated everyone had already left for the day. He turned left, passed the reception desk, then moved right toward Jeff Levon's office. As he approached the door, he heard muffled voices inside. He couldn't decipher everything, but he thought he recognized Doug's voice.

"Is everything squared away with Brian?"

"Not yet. There's a bit of a back-up in the paperwork, so he'll have to be processed tomorrow along with the other two."

"I don't like it. We need to manage these people faster. We can't have them hanging around. If we're caught – "

"Don't get your panties in a bunch, Doug. No one will get caught. Besides, even if we did, the client will take care of it, as always."

"I know, I know. But still..."

Paul tiptoed away from Jeff's office, then around the next corner. While puzzling over the conversation, he heard Jeff's office door open, and Doug and Jeff's voices floated toward him. He ran to the end of the hall, and entered a door marked simply HR. He quietly shut and locked it, leaning his ear against the cool wood as he waited in the dark. Doug and Jeff must have gone the other way because Paul couldn't hear them anymore.

His ragged breathing echoed in his ears, and he took a

few moments to calm down. His eyes slowly adjusted to the dark room as he felt along the wall for the light switch. He bumped into something on his right. It felt like a garment bag, and it swung back and forth, heavy with something inside. It must have hung from a chain because there was an eerie clanking noise with each movement. A quiet whispering sound, that he couldn't quite place, replaced the sound of Paul's heavy breathing. He reached out to stop the object's motion, and immediately regretted it. The shape felt too familiar.

He backed up, his left hand reaching for the wall for support. He found the light switch by accident and, dreading what lay in front of him but desperate to know all the same, he flipped the switch. The glare of the overhead light blinded him for a moment. When his eyes adjusted, he stared at Brian Rollins. Brian's body was in a clear body bag that hung from what looked like a hotel luggage cart. His throat had been slit, blood painted the inside of the bag in thick streaks. There were two other bodies hanging beside him. Paul recognized one of them, Sherman Hall, who quit two days ago. The bags were rubbing together, creating the eerie whispering sound.

He shook his head from side to side, moaning in horror and disgust. He looked around the room, desperate for an indication of why these men were here, and he noticed a small door in the far wall. It was metal, about a three-foot square, with a locking latch at the top. Paul approached it cautiously, reaching for the handle. It opened to a chute, similar to what apartment tenants use to dump their garbage. The metal was warm, but not hot. Was this attached to a furnace?

He looked at the wall around the chute, and saw a sign consisting of two words, posted above it. He released the chute door, and it slammed loudly back into place. His arms fell slack, and his legs collapsed beneath him. Sliding down to the floor, Paul crumpled into a heap. He could hear footsteps approaching. Someone called, trying to open the door, but he didn't care.

He gaped up at the sign above the chute. The "H" and the "R" were in large capital letters, and the black print filled his vision in its neatness and simplicity. He understood what happened to the people who were fired. He knew where his coworkers went when they quit. He had discovered why no one ever kept in touch once they left the company. The client hated to lose anyone to the competition, and worried that those who left might leak confidential information. So, the firm had come up with the perfect solution. No one was allowed to leave alive. Ever.

The Human Removal department saw to that.

RUN

She lifted her skirt to look at her right leg. A tear in the nylons ran from her knee to her ankle, beginning and ending with quarter-sized holes.

"Now, look what you've done."

She backhanded the diminutive man, her submissive for the next thirty-seven minutes. Though he paid for a full hour, she just couldn't take it anymore. He was the third client today who'd ripped her pantyhose. *The fucking things didn't grow on trees, goddammit.*

She strode to the windows facing the bustling street outside of her apartment, and opened the far-left one. Walking back to her client, the little man held up his hands, and shook his head. She ground her teeth, and spoke through a clenched jaw.

"I warned you once before, Patrick."

"I'm sorry! It'll never happen again, I swear."

"I know."

She picked him up, carried him to the open window, and tossed him out. She could hear him scream as he fell all five floors to the sidewalk, where his shouts came to a sudden and wet end.

Wiping her hands together, she moved to the wall phone. She pushed the intercom button, and spoke.

"Cheryl, can you cancel my next two appointments? I've got to run out and get more nylons."

"Again? Please tell me you disciplined that little shit."

Her eyes slid toward the window, "Yes, he won't be doing it again."

"All right. I'll make some calls."

"Thanks, Cheryl. I'll be back in a bit."

One of the sheer curtains flapped in the afternoon breeze coming through the open window. There was a little nip in the air, and she hummed as she gathered her purse and coat, then headed out the door.

SHATTERED

Nothing here is real.
The people, the tables and chairs,
Even the walls.
Their stained softness can't hold me.
The white coats tell me different.
But they aren't real.
Bugs in the food, fire in the halls.
They don't bother me. They're not real.
These wings on my back, the rusty
Scales on my arms. Not real.
Not.
Real.
I am real, though
I don't feel the pinch of needles.
Sensations of hot and cold are lost.
All the people here pay me no mind.
Maybe I'm the one who's not real.
Am I
Not
Real?

SWIFT

"Ssshh, it'll all be over soon."

The whimpering intensified from behind the gag. Wide, wet eyes stared into his before they looked to the eight-inch boning knife in his hand. As he brought it to her throat, she took one last inhale, then he pulled the blade across her pale flesh.

She bucked against the restraints. Soft clicks emanated from the gaping wound as she sucked in air. He put the knife back on the altar, and picked up a shining, silver bowl. Pressing it under the flow of blood, he smoothed damp hair away from her sweaty brow. The bowl filled with fluid, and her eyelids drooped. He wiped spilled tears from her cheeks.

"It'll all be over soon."

After her head fell forward, he turned back to the altar. He grabbed a pristine, white cloth, then wiped the smudged blood off the edge of the bowl. He placed the towel to the side, and the bowl in front of the framed picture of his ex-wife. All he needed to do now was light seven candles (one for each year of their marriage,) dip the carved effigy into the blood, and set it aflame. He glared at the photo.

"It'll all be over soon."

BENDING SPACE

"I had the weirdest dream."

"What was it this time?"

Cheryl smiled at her roommate. "Well, you know how I always try that astral projection stuff – "

"And never succeed, yes."

"Same thing last night, but once I fell asleep, I dreamed I was moving around like I would with projecting."

Roberta finished buttering her toast and crammed a corner of the bread in her mouth, tearing off a large piece. "And?" she muffled.

"So, I'm floating around upstairs, too chicken to move out the window, then I head down to the kitchen. And at the bottom of the stairs, right on that wall – "

Cheryl pointed at the narrow section of wall between the railing and the grandfather clock. "I saw the words 'Be Careful' written out, like in pen or pencil."

Roberta stopped chewing and dropped the uneaten toast on a plate. Cheryl thought she was about to make fun of her, but Roberta's eyes shone with uneasiness.

"Roberta, are you all right?"

Her roommate finally swallowed, and got up from her seat at the table. She moved to the bottom of the stairs and pointed at the wall.

"Are you sure this is where you saw the words?"

"Well, yeah. Roberta, what's going on?"

Roberta turned and looked up the stairs, toward the second-floor landing. She spoke without turning around.

"You know how this house makes that weird sound when you open the back door?"

"Yeah, like a pressure change."

"Exactly. I heard that last night. It woke me up, but when nothing else happened, I thought I imagined it. Then, I swear I heard someone moving around in the kitchen. I jumped out of bed, grabbed my bat, and waited as I heard steps move here, to the foot of the stairs. After a minute of quiet, I started to open my door to go check it out, but it sounded like the back door opened, and everything was quiet again."

Cheryl gaped at her rommate's back, then stared at the wall.

Roberta turned her head to look at the same space. "I figured I dreamed the whole thing and went back to sleep."

She reached out to touch the wall when a small picture of the two of them at graduation crashed to the floor. Roberta froze, her hand inches from the nail where the picture had hung only seconds before.

Cheryl screamed, then laughed at her skittishness. "Holy crap that scared me."

Roberta grinned, but otherwise hadn't moved. Her brow knitted in a frown as she stared at the now empty wall. She leaned forward and studied the paint below the nail.

"Cheryl, does that look funny to you?"

"What do you mean?"

"Like the paint is cracked or something."

Cheryl stepped forward as Roberta lowered her hand. She squinted, tilted her head, then stepped back.

"Maybe the picture scratched it when it fell."

"I suppose."

Cheryl shrugged it off and sat back at the kitchen table, but Roberta studied the wall, seemingly unconvinced of the coincidence between Cheryl's dream, her sudden waking in the night, and now the fallen photograph. She bent down to pick it up, then turned it over. The hook built into the frame was twisted out of shape, as if someone took a pair of pliers to the thin metal, and destroyed it.

Three nights later, Roberta awoke with a start. She sat up in bed, fear pounding in time with her rapid heartbeat. She didn't know why, but Roberta felt Cheryl was in danger. She bolted out of bed, and ran to her roommate's room.

Pounding on the door, she shouted. "Cheryl? Cheryl, wake up!"

Roberta heard a loud thump and a muffled "oof" from Cheryl's room. Not waiting, Roberta opened the door to find Cheryl on the floor, rubbing her knee.

She frowned. "What the hell happened, Roberta?"

"You tell me."

Cheryl rubbed her eyes. "Well, I think I was having another astral projection dream, like before, but this time it felt different. More – "

"More real?"

"Yeah. I floated around the house for a bit, then I was near the ceiling, looking down at my bed. When you pounded on my door, it's like I was thrown back in my body, and the force knocked me onto the floor."

"Did you do anything while you were...out?"

Cheryl smiled. "Yeah. I stacked a bunch of glasses on the kitchen counter but – "

Roberta hurried out of Cheryl's room, and ran down to the kitchen. On the counter next to the sink, stood a small pyramid of six drinking glasses. She stared at them, gently dragging her finger along the structure to make sure it was real. Cheryl came down the stairs, and stood next to Roberta.

"Holy shit. That wasn't a dream, I guess."

Roberta turned to Cheryl. "Did you consciously make the decision to do this, or were you just going along with it being a dream?"

Cheryl frowned. "I think I tried to direct my dream, you know? Or at least what I thought was a dream."

Roberta nodded. "Seems like your practice is finally paying off. Maybe you should stop for a while."

"Are you kidding? This means I'm finally getting the hang of it."

Cheryl turned and ran back upstairs, shouting as she went. "Let's see what else I can do!"

It was no use trying to talk her out of it. Roberta stared at the glasses, and a frosty tendril of air crawled across her shoulders. As she hugged herself against the sudden chill, the top glass on the pyramid teetered, then fell into the sink, shattering into pieces. She spun around, searching the kitchen, as if she knew someone was standing behind her. The feeling quickly passed, but she ran back up to her room, and buried herself under the covers.

The next morning, Roberta's alarm screeched to life. She slapped her hand aimlessly around her nightstand until she connected with the clock. The bell quieted, and Roberta rubbed the sleep from her eyes. As she yawned, she felt...something close in. Opening her eyes, Roberta saw Cheryl standing over her, inches from her nose. Screaming, Roberta scrambled out from beneath her blankets, and sat up against her headboard.

"What the hell, Cheryl? Why are you – "

Cheryl's body shimmered, like a heat wave off blacktop. Roberta pulled her comforter up to her chin.

"Cheryl?"

The visage didn't change or move, aside from the rhythmic shiver, but her eyes followed Roberta's every move as she tried to push away from Cheryl's image. Scooching along the headboard, keeping her blankets between the two of them for some semblance of protection, Roberta slipped out of bed, and inched toward her door. Cheryl watched her, her body slowly turning to follow, and she smiled.

Opening her bedroom door, Roberta yelled down the hall. "Cheryl?"

She didn't take her eyes off her roommate's image as she called again. "Cheryl? Wake up!"

Floating Cheryl smiled, her mouth opening with a silent laugh. She winked at Roberta, then popped out of existence. Half a minute later, Cheryl's bedroom door opened, and she shuffled toward Roberta, smiling.

"Morning, roomie."

Roberta stared at her, waiting to see if this was another projection. But when the shimmer didn't come, Roberta blew out a long breath, and folded her arms across her chest.

"What the hell, Cheryl? You scared the shit out of me."

Cheryl shrugged. "Sorry about that. I wasn't even sure you'd be able to see me."

She didn't sound sorry, but Roberta decided not to press the issue. "Well, I could. How long were you watching me like that?"

"Just a minute or two. No biggie. Let's go see if anything worked."

"Anything? What else did you get up to?"

Cheryl turned, and went downstairs. As Roberta grabbed her thick, fluffy robe, she heard a yell of triumph. She made her way down to the kitchen, and stopped on the last step. Every dish, glass, utensil, and piece of cookware had been taken out of their respective drawers and cabinets, and strewn all over the floor. There was hardly an open spot to step as Roberta watched Cheryl maneuver through it all. She smiled up at her.

"Oh my God, I can't believe this was all real! I can't wait to try again when I get home from work."

"Uh, you're gonna clean all this up first, right?"

"No time. I'm already late, but you work from home. You can do it, right?"

Cheryl hopped through the mess to the stairs, then ran up to her room, calling over her shoulder. "Thanks, roomie!"

Roberta stared back at the kitchen, then closed her eyes. She took three deep, long breaths before surveying the damage. As she began mumbling curses, plaguing Cheryl with 1000 nicks from a razor, she studied the far-right corner of the kitchen floor.

While most everything looked random, the utensils in that section formed some sort of pattern. She tiptoed her way over, only stubbing her toe twice on a large sauce pot and casserole dish. Resisting the urge to kick them in frustration, she stood over the pile of utensils, squinting. The dull, grey morning left the kitchen in gloom, so she shuffled to the light switch, and flicked it on.

Bright white spilled across the floor, and Roberta could make out the pattern from her position. The utensils spelled out the word "STOP." Frowning, Roberta wondered why Cheryl would have done that. Unless she didn't. But if not her, then who? She looked back at the wall at the foot of the stairs, and the framed picture of the two of them. A crack in the glass spread from one corner to the other.

What the hell was happening?

Despite what happened with the "word by cutlery" – Cheryl hadn't done it, that she remembered – the cracked picture, and the stone of fear lodged in Roberta's chest, Cheryl continued her AP adventures every night. The more adept she got at maneuvering and affecting the real world, the stronger, and more sinister, the warnings got. Different words scratched into the dry wall and wood; a small fire started in a trash can in the bathroom; a dead bird stuffed under Cheryl's pillow.

None of that, nor Roberta's increasing fear, stopped or even slowed Cheryl's practice. Roberta tried to reason with her one night as they readied for bed.

"Cheryl, don't you think it's odd that you're actually affecting the physical world when you project? That's not supposed to happen, is it?"

She shrugged. "Maybe no one else has been as good at it as I am."

Roberta almost lost her jaw as it dropped in disbelief. "Really? No one, among the thousands of people who've practiced over thousands of years, has been good enough at it?"

"Yeah, why not?"

"Why not? Are you seriously that arrogant, or just extremely delusional?"

Cheryl frowned as she stared at Roberta's reflection in

the bathroom mirror. Roberta held the dental floss between two back teeth as Cheryl offered a predatory smirk.

"Be careful, Bert. I can mess with all sorts of stuff besides the Tupperware."

Roberta stared at the back of Cheryl's head as she walked out into the hall. When her roommate's door closed with a soft click, Roberta swallowed, then threw out the floss. She realized she had no way of protecting herself from whatever machinations AP Cheryl would get up to in the night.

"Looks like you won't be getting much sleep," Roberta said to her reflection.

Roberta went to her room, and before she closed the door, Cheryl opened hers a crack, reaching out to wiggle her fingers. "Night-night, roomie. Sweet dreams."

She giggled, then closed her door. Goosebumps popped up across Roberta's arms as she locked herself in her room. She knew it wouldn't keep AP Cheryl out for long, but her survival instincts had already kicked in and taken over. She also pushed her vanity chair under the knob, left the ceiling light on, and turned on her bedside lamp.

Maybe she should make some coffee to help with her night-long vigil. Cheryl couldn't have gotten into projection mode already, so now might be her only chance.

Prepped with a full pot of java, a laptop filled with downloaded movies and tv shows, Roberta felt she'd be able to stay awake the whole night, just in case. *In case what?* Could she really prevent Cheryl from getting in if Cheryl was determined to do it? Roberta shook her head. If she went down that road, she'd die of fright long before Cheryl had a chance to do anything.

Sipping from her first cup, Roberta put a sitcom on the screen, and settled back against her headboard. Gripping the mug, she bolstered her confidence with an internal pep talk.

"You got this. You can do this. You survived four older brothers and an alcoholic mom. This is like a cake walk. Yeah, you're good. You're good."

Several hours later, Roberta woke with a start. Her laptop flashed the DVD's main menu choices, and her empty cup lay on the bed next to her. The half-filled coffee pot, now cold, sat on her nightstand, mocking her. She caught movement from the corner of her eye, and turned to see Floating Cheryl at the foot of the bed. Roberta gasped, but Cheryl held up her hands, not in aggression, but in appeasement.

Her mouth moved, but no sound came out. Cheryl pulled her hair in frustration, then pointed at the door with one hand, beckoning Roberta with the other.

"Cheryl, what's wrong?"

She continued to gesture, then reached forward to grab Roberta's arm. But before she could, it looked like an unseen force yanked Cheryl backward. She pointed again, and Roberta slipped out of bed.

"Is there something wrong in your room?"

Cheryl bobbed her head up and down, then moved through Roberta's open door. Cheryl really could manipulate anything in this plane, but Roberta refused to think about it as she went out to the hall and into Cheryl's room, where the door stood open.

Roberta noted Cheryl's empty bed. She looked between it and her roommate's floating form.

"Where are you, Cheryl?"

She shook her head, splaying her hands and shrugging.

"Okay, so you're not in here. Have you checked anywhere else?"

She shook her head again, then pointed at Roberta.

"You just came to me first, looking for help."

Cheryl nodded, mouthing the word, "roomie," before a small smile curled her lips.

"Interesting. First you threaten me, now you need my help."

The smile fell away, replaced with an angry grimace. She reached out to grab Roberta, and managed to brush against her pj's, before being pulled away by the invisible force again.

"Good to know this predicament has put things in perspective for you. So, if I were your body, where would I go?"

Cheryl waited while Roberta chewed on her fingernail. "Hmmm, maybe the kitchen. We both know how much you enjoy messing around in there."

She walked down to the kitchen, but no Cheryl-body waited. "Maybe the basement? The booze is down there."

Roberta offered Floating Cheryl a smirk, then walked downstairs. The low-watt bulbs snapped to life, but only to reveal shelves of knick-knacks, an old buffet table holding their modest alcohol stash, and bits and pieces of mismatched, inherited furniture.

But no body.

"Well, shit. Where the hell are you?"

Moving back through the kitchen, Roberta then walked the entire first floor, checking every spare room, bathroom, closet, storage cabinet, or anywhere Cheryl could fit. Standing in the back bedroom, she scratched her head, completely stumped, when a low rumble echoed from outside.

She cocked her head then turned to Floating Cheryl. "Is that a car?"

Cheryl's eye widened as she shook her head. She moved through the house to the back door, and Roberta followed. Cheryl hovered at the door, looking helpless.

Roberta frowned. "Can't you open it?"

Floating Cheryl shook her head.

"Something must be wrong. We'd better get outside, quick."

Roberta burst through the door and out into the yard. Floating Cheryl followed, and they both stopped at the side of the garage. A dull light shone from under the narrow door. Roberta pressed her nose against the smudgy window and saw a cloud of exhaust enveloping Cheryl's car as the engine rumbled. Cheryl's body sat in the driver's seat, slumped over the steering wheel.

"Oh my God, Cheryl!"

Roberta rattled the doorknob, but it wouldn't turn. She banged on the door, and threw her weight against it, but no luck. She'd have to break the glass. As she turned to find a brick or heavy rock, Floating Cheryl reached toward the knob, and somehow forced it to turn, and the door popped open. Her apparition sagged as if exhausted. *How the hell was she doing that?* Roberta could worry about the intricacies of true astral projection later. Right now, she had to get Cheryl's body out of that car.

She entered the garage, immediately waving her hands in front of her face to clear some of the fumes. All the car windows were open, and she thrust the top half of her body through the driver's side. Gently moving Cheryl away from the wheel, Roberta twisted around to the side and turned the car key to "off," and the engine ceased its rumbling. Pulling open the door, Roberta lifted Cheryl's body from the car, and dragged her out into the night air.

"As soon as we get you inside, the house *and* your body, we need to talk, Cheryl."

Roberta struggled with Cheryl's dead weight, but managed to get her back inside quickly. She lay her on the living room couch, and covered her with a thin blanket. Grabbing the phone on the end table, Roberta started to dial 9-1-1, but Floating Cheryl waved her arms to stop her.

"What? Cheryl, you need medical help."

Cheryl motioned to her floating form, then pointed at her body.

"I guess you can't wake up unless you're in there, huh?"

Cheryl nodded, and Roberta put the phone down. She pointed at Floating Cheryl.

"Get in your body right now. I'll give you thirty seconds to wake up on your own, then I'm calling an ambulance."

Cheryl smiled, and drifted above her body. She slowly turned to face the ceiling, then lowered herself down to the couch. Once Floating Cheryl melded with Physical Cheryl, Roberta began to count.

"One. Two. Three. Four."

She got to twenty-seven before Cheryl bolted upright, sucking in a huge gasp of air. She expelled in it a fit of coughing. Roberta ran to get a glass of water. By the time she'd returned, Cheryl's coughing had subsided. She took the water and gulped it down. Roberta rubbed a hand across her back.

"Better?"

"Yeah, thanks."

"Cheryl – "

"Just give me a minute."

"Cheryl, after what happened tonight, you may not have a minute."

"I know. Just let me drink a little more."

Roberta let her take a few more sips, but didn't wait for her to speak. "We need to talk about this. I'm not exactly sure what's going on, but even I know what you're doing isn't astral projection."

Cheryl nodded. "You're right. It's not. As I was researching AP, I found this off-shoot, like an underground cult, of what's known as EP – Energy Projection. You don't just let your ethereal consciousness go on a walk-about. You send a physical manifestation of your energy."

"Why? To what end?"

She shrugged. "To affect the world around you while your body stays safe. Maybe just for shits and giggles."

"Shits and giggles? Is this a game to you?"

Cheryl shrugged again. "I don't know. Maybe."

"Well, someone doesn't appreciate your sense of humor. You were warned, several times, and now this happened."

"Yeah, I guess I pissed someone off."

"Ya think? You need to stop now before it's too late."

"Are you kidding? No way. I can take better precautions. I can protect myself better from now on."

"How? Are you gonna lock your body up in some bank vault? What if the person warning you is also a fan of EP? Where can you hide from that?"

"I don't know, but I'm not stopping. I'm having too much fun. And I've almost – "

She stopped then looked away.

"Almost what, Cheryl? You're not just doing this for fun. You're up to something. Tell me."

"I can't. Not yet."

Roberta stood, and threw her hands up in the air. "Fine. Do whatever you want, Cheryl. You always do. But don't expect me to sit around and watch you get yourself killed."

Roberta stomped off through the kitchen and back

upstairs. She could hear Cheryl begin to cry, but somehow she knew it was an act. When Cheryl must have thought Roberta was out of earshot, she mumbled, and Roberta heard it loud and clear. Maybe she wanted Roberta to hear.

"I don't need you anyway, bitch."

Roberta went to her room, and slammed the door. She texted her aunt, selfishly hoping the older woman's insomnia was in full-swing tonight, to see if she could stay with her for a while. No way was Roberta going to live with some psycho whose cheese had almost completely slid off her cracker. Cheryl had already messed with, and threatened, her. As far as Roberta was concerned, their friendship was done.

As she pulled out her suitcase and started to pack, Roberta heard Cheryl come up the stairs and stop outside in the hall. Roberta waited for a knock that never came. She stopped packing and stared at the shadow beneath the door. The knob rattled, then slowly turned. Shock widened Roberta's eyes as the door creaked open to reveal Cheryl standing there, arms folded, with a smirk on her face.

Roberta noted the sheen of sweat across Cheryl's brow, and the tremble in her body.

It was Roberta's turn to smirk. "After your adventure with Captain Carbon Monoxide, I'm guessing that's all you can muster right now. Nice parlor trick, but if you don't mind, I'm kinda busy."

She strode to the door, and slammed it in Cheryl's face. Her roommate's heavy breath hovered out in the hall for a moment before Cheryl stomped off to her own room, screaming, "Fine!" before slamming her door. Roberta dropped the sweater she'd been holding and bent over, resting her hands on her knees, and almost started hyperventilating. Her bravado was just that. She'd never felt more scared in her life. She needed to get out of here before Cheryl regained her strength.

Within half an hour, Roberta's aunt replied to her text, saying she had plenty of room to spare. After getting that confirmation, Roberta scanned her room. She'd packed most of her clothes, laptop, some pictures and random possessions. She just needed to get her toiletries from the bathroom, and she would get the hell out of Dodge.

She cracked open her bedroom door, hoping all would be quiet and Floating Cheryl-free. But she wasn't prepared for what she saw. An intense, blue light shone from underneath Cheryl's door. It was so bright, it lit up the entire top floor. A low humming noise, that Roberta felt as much as heard, emanated from Cheryl's room. Pictures on the walls shook, and some crashed to the floor. The door frame to the bathroom fractured, then zig-zag cracks tore through part of the surrounding wall.

"Fuck you, Colgate. I can get more at the drug store."

Roberta grabbed her suitcase and purse, and snagged her favorite stuffed rabbit off her bed. Though she was still in her pj's, she ran down the stairs, out the back door, and threw everything into her car as fast as she could. When she'd backed her car to the end of the driveway, a flash of white broke through the darkness as Cheryl's bedroom windows blew out.

Roberta screamed, and punched the accelerator, rocketing her car down the street.

A month later, after the police stopped asking questions, when the local tv station interview requests stopped coming, when everyone wrote off Cheryl's disappearance with the strange lights and cacophony as coincidence,

Roberta was enjoying a quiet summer night on the screened-in back porch. Her aunt never pestered her with questions, never hinted at wanting Roberta to get on with her life and find a place of her own. Which was good because, in all honesty, Roberta was still afraid to be alone. She could hear the tv in the living room, her aunt watching reruns of *Murder, She Wrote*, and Roberta smiled.

As she sipped some hot tea, the porch door thumped, as if someone tried to open it. Roberta held the tea cup just below her lip as her eyes shifted to the right. The old metal screen popped open, and the glass door shook again.

"...Bert..."

A tinny voice, like an echo through a coffee can, sounded from outside. As she stared, the soft outline of a person formed on the other side of the door. Though faint, and just a shadow of her past projections, Cheryl's image coalesced in the dark. Roberta dropped the cup, and it bounced on the low pile carpet, darkening it with spilled tea. She shot up from her chair, and started backing away.

"...Bert, wait. I won't hu..."

Her voice wavered in and out, chopping her sentences into fragments.

"...ning out...time..."

Roberta inched forward. Cheryl's image flickered, but remained outside. Whatever she had been up to, clearly her "powers" were not as strong as they once were. Roberta reached the door, laying her hand on the metal latch. Cheryl backed away, and offered a smile.

As Roberta stepped outside, Floating Cheryl clenched her fists, and squeezed her eyes closed. Roberta almost ran back inside, but while she watched, Cheryl's image deepened, became more opaque, almost solid. When she opened her eyes, Cheryl's expression was one of fear, and sadness.

"Roberta, I don't have much time. I'm getting weaker. Soon, I'll be gone entirely."

"Cheryl, what – ?"

"The warnings – they weren't for me. They were for you."

"Me?"

"I was asking you to stop me. I needed you to stop me."

"I don't understand."

Her image flickered for a moment, chopping up her sentences again.

"I broke through...time continuu..."

"You did what?" Roberta shouted, not even sure if Cheryl could hear her.

"...stop me. Why didn't...stop me?"

Her voice cracked with panic, her image blinking out completely for a few seconds before reappearing.

"...broke the law...angry with me..."

"Who is? What's going on?"

Cheryl turned to look behind her. Roberta leaned to side, but didn't see anything, and realized she never would. Cheryl was somewhere else, some place she didn't belong, and Roberta couldn't help her.

Not now. It was too late.

Cheryl looked at Roberta, and reached out. Her voice, fading, spiraling farther and farther away, pleaded one last time.

"Why didn't you stop me?"

Her form vanished, like a popped balloon, her terrified voice cut off mid-shriek. The night sat quiet around Roberta. No crickets, no wind, absolute silence as she stared at the empty space before her.

POISON

Your skin, shaded blue.
Foaming spittle from your mouth.
Just die already.

SWORD

"I will not let you destroy this, Jeannine."

thunk

"I will not let you destroy my happiness."

shunk

"I will NOT let you destroy me!"

He rammed the last sword into the back of her neck. Her squirming had stopped a long time ago. She'd probably died when the fifth sword was thrust between her L1 and L2 vertebrae. The tarot reader didn't specify exactly what disaster was headed his way, but he already knew. Jeannine was going to take everything – the house, the car, their savings – and worst of all, the children. He could live without the rest, but Suzie and Jacob meant everything to him. He couldn't allow her to steal them.

Perhaps by recreating that dreaded card, the one that came up in the "future" spot at his reading, he could negate its power. The psychic told him it was useless. The Ten of Swords always indicated inevitable disaster.

Fuck that.

As he stepped back and studied his work, he could already feel the darkness that had clouded his brain begin to lift. The sharp, coppery smell of blood opened his sinuses, and he breathed deep.

Yeah. Things were going to be just fine.

TEEMING

As his head slipped beneath the writhing surface, the hundreds of millipedes crawling into his ears, nose, and mouth, he realized he should have taken that left turn at Alberquerque.

UNDERWATER

The young girl looked down at her reflection in the pond. But unlike the hundreds of lazy afternoons she'd done it before, this time her reflection didn't match. When she tilted her head to the right, it tilted left. When she smiled, it frowned. Even her hair, which hung in blonde ringlets around her head, differed from the dark tresses of the image, which were pulled back into a tight, high ponytail.

"Who are you?" she asked the reflection.

"I'm you, silly," it said.

"Well, if you're me, does that mean I'm you?"

It shook its head slowly. Glowing, red eyes rose through the water; sharp, taloned fingers broke the surface, and grabbed her hair. It snarled and spit as clear, viscous jelly dripped from its needle teeth.

"You're nobody."

The creature pulled the terrified girl into the water, her struggles barely making a splash. Within minutes, it was as if she'd never existed at all, save for one lone ripple that disturbed the pond's smooth, glassy surface.

HOMECOMING

I miss you. I miss the days when I was a little girl, and you would tuck me in at night, shooing away the monsters from under the bed and out of my closet. When you came home from a long exhausting day of work, managing a small and charming stationery store, though weary, you always had a smile for me. You'd pick me up, squeeze me tight, kiss my cheek, and tell me you missed me. That you loved me.

I even miss the jealousy you roused in mom. The sidelong glances, the twitch of her mouth, the small wrinkled frown she thought I couldn't see as she turned away, pretending to cook dinner or tuck a strand of hair behind her ear. She hid so much from you. But not from me.

There was no denying the truth about the back of her hand against my cheek. Or the crack of my neck when she yanked my hair, dragging me to the little closet beneath the stairs. Every bruise could be explained away (remember how klutzy I was during grade school?) and each sore muscle was hidden behind my smiles.

How could I tell you the truth? How could I break your

heart as you embraced the woman you loved, kissed her under the mistletoe, swung her around in your arms as she squealed with delight? You had everything you wanted, and deserved. I loved you too much to shatter your perfect world.

In fact, I would gladly spend 1000 more hours in that cramped hellhole if it meant I could hear your voice again, your breath warm against my ear. I would endure the beatings, humiliations, any and all abuse she could dream up if I'd be able to feel your arms around me, and the scratch of your weekend stubble tickling my neck. I would do anything to see you again.

Anything.

Maybe you wouldn't approve of that. Maybe you'd shake your head at me, clucking your tongue, and tell me the mess isn't worth it. You might be right. Perhaps slitting mom's throat from ear to ear doesn't solve anything. But who else's blood could I mix with your grave dirt? Who else deserved to die to give you life again? It's too late anyway. It's already done. All I have to do now is wait, wait for you to return to me.

Daddy, come home.

GOT YER NOSE

John crept down the stairs, holding his baseball bat at the ready. He'd always kept one by his bed, ever since the night Harry the Strongman snuck into John's trailer with the intent of pounding his head into oatmeal. Apparently, Harry never had anyone, let alone a lowly knife thrower, steal a woman right out from under his nose before.

After retiring from the big top circuit, John found this tenement house. All of the other borders were ex-circus folk, too. Seemed even after the traveling cirky lifestyle ended, they all still circled one another, creating their cliques and groups, and no one outside "the life" was allowed to enter.

As he got to the bottom of the steps, John heard it again, the sound that woke him from a dead sleep just a few minutes earlier.

Squeak.

John racked his brain, trying to match up the sound with some long-forgotten slot in his memory bank, but it just wouldn't come. All he knew was it didn't belong here, especially at three in the morning. He had to find out what it was, make sure everyone was safe. Although never official, John made himself the protector of this retirement community, and none of the other residents ever tried to convince him otherwise.

He moved to the living room, and at first glance, saw nothing out of place. The streetlamp on the corner shone its full yellow light over the ragged, but comfortable, easy chair, the plastic seat covers on the couch, the flat, dull surface of the television, and all the various knick-knacks and tchotchkes on the tables and shelves. Everything looked normal except...

There. Off to the left, at the base of the television. A round ball, its color faded and pale, stood out against the dark wood floor. John frowned as he walked over. He reached for it, his aged knees popping, and his sore back forcing an involuntary groan from his mouth as he bent over.

Standing again, he held the ball up to the light streaming in through the window. He squinted at it.

"What the hell? It looks like," he stopped mid sentence. He felt his eyes widen in shock. *It couldn't be. It just couldn't.*

He thought back to a hot, muggy night twenty years earlier. Too much booze and not enough restraint; lingering anger over an imagined insult; a prank gone horribly wrong; and the smell of blood. Lots of blood.

The lamp on the end table to his right snapped on. He jerked his head in its direction. In the corner, which moments before only held shadows, stood a clown. Its baggy jumpsuit sagged in sad folds, the colored polka-dots faded as if sun-bleached, and the white background dingy with age. Grease paint had been left to dry and flake off the clown's face, leaving smears of powdery white, blue, yellow, and red to stand out in stark contrast against the grey flesh underneath.

Its dull purple shoes, the color of dying lilacs, and five sizes larger than the man's real feet, tapped alternately in a rhythm of a song John couldn't hear. At least, not out loud. But he knew the melody well, had heard it every day of his life for thirty years. The tinny music of the calliope rang loud and clear, playing "Entrance of the Gladiators," over and over in his head.

All that didn't unnerve John. Despite its unusual presence, even here, there were only two things about the clown that scared him. First, was the face. Instead of a red, round nose, a black, oozing crater sat in the center of its features, the flesh of the opening ragged and torn. And second, he knew who the clown was, or rather, who he *had* been when he was still alive.

John looked down at the faded, squishy orb in his hand, and realized it was the clown's nose. He dropped it in disgust, and it let out a small squeak when it hit the floor.

That sound. That's where he had heard it before. He turned to look back at the intruder. The last thing John saw was a flash of curly orange hair, and a torn and dirty white glove, as it reached for him. The bat slipped from John's hand, and fell on the bulbous nose.

Squeak.

DEAD AND BURIED?

I killed her today.
Buried her out off Route 10
In the abandoned mill.
So why can I still smell
Her perfume?
Why can I still hear
Her voice?
Footsteps in the hall
Behind me.
Light.
Delicate.
Feminine.
A clump of quick-drying cement
Rolls past my foot.
I know, because that's what I
Poured over the body.
The pale ashen skin of the
Hand on my shoulder
Is scraped and bloody.
Several nails are cracked, broken,

Or gone.
A brush of tangled hair caresses
My cheek as she whispers
In my ear.
'My love.'
I should dig a deeper hole
Next time.

CASUALTY OF WAR

David poked at his captive as she swung back and forth. He had restrained her arms in a cocoon of rope, and suspended her from a heavy metal hook in the ceiling. Rubbing his cheek where she had kicked him, he smiled.

"I have to admit I was somewhat impressed with your defensive skills. But my stun gun proved more effective."

Laughing, David walked over to a small metal table covered with a thick blue cloth. He flipped off the fabric with a majestic flourish revealing an array of syringes, droppers, basters, and spray bottles. He picked up a large plastic bucket from the floor, heavy with liquid, and placed it on the table.

"Now, Amelia, we're going to play a game. It's called 'Twenty Questions'. I'm going to ask you twenty questions and if you don't give me the answers I want–"

He picked up one of the basters, pointed it at her, then squeezed the plastic bulb. A puff of air hit her in the face, and she flinched. She looked back at the bucket, and her skin quivered with fear.

"What's in there?"

David plunged the tip of the baster into the container and filled it with the clear liquid. "In here? Nothing, really."

He tipped the baster into his mouth and emptied it. He swished the fluid between his cheeks before swallowing.

"Just water."

Amelia's eyes went wide in terror. "Why are you doing this? I've never done anything to you."

David grabbed a syringe and filled it from the bucket. He approached Amelia, and yanked off one of her shoes. He plunged the needle into the top of her foot. She screamed in agony as a bright golden flame seared her flesh, following the route of the water as it traveled up the vein in her leg. It slowed and finally died out, leaving a long-blackened scab that marred her flaky skin.

He refilled the syringe, then grabbed her other foot, pulled off that shoe, and held the needle above it in warning. Amelia stopped squirming, but anger lit up her eyes. They shifted from brown to orange then yellow before returning to their original color.

"First question. What are you?"

Amelia pressed her lips together and said nothing. David stabbed the needle into her foot, and pushed the plunger. She howled in pain again as the water burned through flesh and bone.

"I repeat, what are you?"

Her breathing quick and shallow, Amelia managed to grunt her response. "A sprite."

"What?" he shouted at her.

"A desert sprite!"

"What are you doing here?"

"I got separated from my clan when we fled to the mountains."

David pushed his face close to hers, their noses almost touching. "I think you're a spy, Amelia."

"No, I'm not. I swear! I got lost, and have been wandering alone in the forest for days."

"You expect me to believe you were on your own that whole time?"

"Yes, that's what I've been trying to tell you."

David narrowed his eyes at her, placed the syringe back on the table, then picked up a spray bottle. He took his time walking around her, squirting thin streams of water randomly onto her body, where her skin would smoke and sizzle. He smiled, enjoying himself at her expense.

"Let's say for one moment that I do believe you, Amelia. Even if you are telling the truth, how do I know you won't run back to your friends and divulge the location of this facility? Perhaps reveal the contents of our stockade, or what I've done to you?"

"I swear, I won't say anything. I got separated from the group, then got lost. That's mostly the truth anyway."

"Mostly?" he whispered into her ear.

Amelia whimpered. David looked down at the collection of implements, and stared at his reflection in the smooth silver surface of the table. Blues and greens of a great ocean tempest swirled in his eyes. He placed the bottle down, then picked up the full bucket of water and faced Amelia. She tried to swing away from him as she screamed.

"I promise I won't tell anyone!"

He chuckled. "I know."

Her eyes flared orange and she growled. "My father was right. Never trust a river nymph. I should have killed you the second I saw you."

"You and what army, sprite?"

Amelia laughed, then jerked her chin at him. "They'll be here soon enough."

David held the bucket against his chest. The corner of his mouth lifted in a cruel sneer.

"That's what's we wanted to confirm, Amelia. I'm afraid they won't be here in time to save you, though."

He threw the water at her, and the room lit up with gold fire as Amelia's flesh burned away to ash. As he waved the heavy smoke from his face, he dropped the bucket, then moved to the corner where he hung his jacket over a squat chair. David grabbed his phone and punched in a series of numbers. After singing a few low notes and clicks at the device, his Captain came on the line.

"Report."

The Overseers would be interested to learn of this sprite infiltration. Over the past few months, the war between their species had grown quiet. The nymphs knew that silence was never a good sign when it came to the cunning and duplicitous nature of sprites. David relayed the afternoon's session to his superior.

"I see," came the reply. "I'll speak to the council about this personally. Are we prepared for further interviews?"

David turned to his right, and stared through the glass window of the interrogation cell at the long open space of the stock room. Hundreds of shelves running the length of the forty thousand square foot area held countless gallon water jugs. The facility could host numerous sessions for years. Thirty-five other warehouses just like it sat at the ready in this city alone.

David hoped the Captain couldn't hear his smile over the phone. "Yes, sir. We're more than ready."

"Good. Carry on."

The Captain broke the connection before David could

reply. He snapped the phone closed, and returned it to his jacket pocket. After reorganizing the torture instruments, and refilling the bucket, he grabbed a small hand broom and began sweeping up the remnants of his enemy. The door behind him opened, and two guards dragged a bruised and dirty sprite into the room.

"Are you all set, sir?"

David gave the prisoner a rudimentary glance as he nodded. "Hang it up like the last one."

They did as instructed, the sprite hissing and cursing the entire time, then left the room. David made a show of brushing the ashy remains into a dustpan, and slowly pouring them into a small garbage can, taking his time to get every last flake into the bin. He watched the captured sprite from the corner of his eye to gauge any reaction. Only when he slammed the pan onto the edge of the container did the creature flinch. He smiled.

David left the cleaning tools near the can, then straightened. As he walked around the hanging creature, he whistled a sweet lullaby his mother used to sing to him as a youngling. The sprite kicked and spun, trying to look at its captor, eyes wide with fear and shining bright yellow. David stood in front of it, and flashed a wide grin. He kicked the bucket of water at its feet.

"Now, sprite. We're going to play a game."

One of the guards outside the interrogation room flinched when the first shriek echoed out into the hallway. The other guard held out his hand, smiling.

"I told you it would be screaming in under five minutes. Pay up."

Grumbling, the first guard dug a small pack containing several vials of blue liquid from a bag snapped onto his belt, and handed it to his comrade who laughed, then put the pack in his shirt pocket. He jerked a thumb over his shoulder.

"He's not called The Thrasher for nothing, you know."

The two guards shared a laugh as the screaming continued.

BURNT TOAST

Flaming ball of gas.
The world spins off its axis.
God shrugs. “Mulligan.”

DOORWAYS

"A door isn't just wood, brass, and metal surrounded by plaster, paint, and glue. It's a barrier between worlds."

"What do you mean, Grandpa?"

Sally looked at the basement door, then back to her grandfather. "What worlds are you talking about?"

"There are two different kinds of worlds, Sally. One we can all see – this kitchen, the living room, and everything outside," he pointed toward the picture window at the front of the house. "You understand what I'm talking about, yes?"

Sally nodded.

"Good. Then there's another world. One that we *can't* see. Well, most of us anyway."

She looked at the cellar door again. "Are you talking about the basement? 'Cause yeah, I can't see it. The door's closed, remember?"

Grandpa shook his head.

"No. I'm talking about another world, other worlds, which exist alongside this one. They're inside this very room, and this house, but sit just out of our line of sight."

He watched his granddaughter as she turned her head left and right, squinting her eyes, as if that would make the invisible plane pop out in front of her. He smiled. So logical, just like her grandmother.

"That's not going to help, Sallyberry Shortcake."

She rolled her eyes at him. "Grandpa, please don't call me that. I'm thirteen. I'm not a baby anymore."

"Right, I forgot. Forgive an old man's memory."

Sally smiled, but her brow furrowed as she looked at him. "Grandpa, do you mean–"

She left her question unasked as she bit her bottom lip. He didn't push, trying to force her thought process. He'd learned over the past thirteen years that Sally did everything in her own time – no sooner, no later.

Sally played with the straw poking up from her glass of iced tea as she spoke. "You're not talking about ghosts, right? Or the afterlife?"

"Nope."

She stuck the straw in her mouth and chewed the end, her eyebrows pushed together like when she concentrated on a difficult math assignment. Darting her eyes left and right, as if worried someone might overhear, Sally leaned forward, then spat out the straw.

"Baymell," she whispered.

He smiled and nodded. "Exactly."

Sally let out a long breath, her face relaxing with relief.

"You though they were a dream, or that maybe you were going crazy, right?"

"Uh huh," she said.

"You thought you'd be like your mother, didn't you?"

"Is that why Mom–"

She let the unasked question hang in the air between them. He took Sally's hands in his own to offer comfort.

"My dear girl, your mother wasn't strong enough. She couldn't accept that place, or them, as real. Could only believe she'd gone mad. That's why she killed herself, Sally. Not because of anything, or anyone, here."

His vision blurred as tears filled his eyes. He blinked them away, and felt them moisten his cheeks. Sally reached out, and wiped his face dry.

"Don't cry, Grandpa. It's okay."

He covered her hands with his own and laughed. "I'll be all right, especially since you understand, about Baymell I mean. How often do you see them?"

"I've only seen them a couple of times so far. And I've been there once."

"What?"

"I went to Baymell. I thought I was dreaming, though."

"Sally, listen to me. You can't ever do that again."

"Why?"

"Things are different over there. Time and space, they don't work the same as here."

"I don't get it."

"I'm saying that it seems like only a few hours or a day passes there but here, it could be weeks or months. Maybe even years."

"That explains a lot."

"What do you mean?"

"Well, when I woke up, I was so tired. I felt like I hadn't slept at all. I guess I didn't, huh?"

"Probably not. What did you do there?"

Sally tilted her head to the side, closing her eyes, as she thought back to her experience.

"They took me to what looked like a huge park – green grass and wildflowers as far as the eyes could see. A bunch of them were running up and down a large hill in the distance, like they were playing tag. Another group was cleaning up what looked like those campfires we used to build when I was little. Remember, Grandpa? When we used to go camping, before Mom got sick."

He grasped Sally's hand as her words trailed off, and tears filled her eyes. "Sick" was how they described her mother's condition. The official diagnosis of paranoid schizophrenia was too complicated to explain to a child. Crazy was a term for the ignorant and bullies of the playground.

"I do, Sally. What else?"

"That's it. One of them was walking toward me, but I woke up before I could talk to him. Actually, you woke me up that morning."

Grandfather frowned. He remembered a few weeks ago, coming down to the kitchen for breakfast, and finding Sally slumped over at the table, sound asleep. Her ghostly pallor and fevered brow indicated she might be getting ill, so he kept her home from school that day. He didn't know then that her sickly appearance was from a trip to Baymell.

"Listen to me very carefully, Sally. You can't ever go there again. If you stay too long, you could become trapped forever. Do you understand me?"

"But–"

"*Do you understand me?*"

"Yes, Grandpa, I do. But what if it happens again while I'm sleeping?"

"Don't worry. I'll watch over you, or keep your door locked so you can't sleep walk to the cellar again."

Sally nodded, then looked up at her grandfather. "Grandpa, is that what happened to Grandma? Did she go over there?"

Sally's grandfather bit his lower lip, and said nothing.

But he didn't have to. His silence told her everything she needed to know.

That night, and for several weeks after, he sat in the rocking chair at the foot of Sally's bed while she slept. When the hard back of the rocker proved too harsh for his aging spine, he locked her bedroom door from the outside. He knew, however, that Sally would venture back to Baymell sooner or later, despite his warnings.

It was what had happened to his wife. The night before she disappeared, they lay in bed, and talked about Baymell and doorways. It's almost as if she knew, as if they both knew, it would be their last night together.

"You know, you leave of piece of yourself behind every time," she'd said.

"What do you mean? In Baymell?"

"Think about it. Whenever a person moves from room to room, one home or building to another, a thread of their energy is left behind. Almost like forensic evidence at a crime scene."

"Okay, I get that."

"It's the same with Baymell," she continued. "Every time I go over, then cross back, a part of me remains there. I suppose that's why it gets easier and easier to return. It's almost like I'm a part of it now."

He clenched his jaw in the darkness. "It calls to you, doesn't it?" he asked.

She grabbed his hand and squeezed. He could hear her trying to hold back the tears and sobs, her breath hitching with the effort. His own tears rolled down his temples and dampened the pillow beneath his head. They eventually fell asleep, wrapped in each other's arms, but he awoke the next morning alone. When he walked down to the kitchen, he found the cellar door ajar, and one of her fuzzy slippers laying at the threshold.

Now, as he rocked back and forth in the chair in Sally's room, he wondered if his plan might work. Could he get his wife back? Would they accept the trade?

At the very least, he hoped they would leave him alone. Over the past few weeks, they'd begun calling to him in his dreams, tempting him with his wife's voice, and the sounds of their games and frivolity. But their world frightened him. The laughter of play sounded like tortured screams, and their music was a rusty calliope, screeching its melody like a feral cat.

Sally rolled over in her sleep with a soft moan. He watched her nestle back into a pile of pillows, pulling the pink floral comforter under her chin. Slowly he stood, the chair and his joints creaking with the sudden changes in position. He tiptoed out of her room, leaving the door open, and snuck into the bathroom across the hall. And there he waited.

He didn't have to wait long. Within minutes, Sally shuffled out of her room, and down the hall. Keeping a safe distance, he followed her through the house to the cellar door. He'd made sure to close it before he put Sally to bed. Somehow the simple act of opening it triggered the portal to Baymell. And now, as he stood behind her, Sally reached for the knob, twisted it, and pulled the door open, the hinges squeaking their protest.

The rush of warm air blew over them bringing with it the scent of rotten fruit, fetid swamp water, mold and slime. Cackles of laughter and screams of horror echoed through the kitchen. And underneath it, he could hear the playful lilt of his wife's voice.

His stomach churned, and he almost vomited. As he got

himself under control, Sally began to move forward. He grabbed the back of her pajama top, and screamed into the portal.

"I know you can hear me. You're not getting my granddaughter. Not unless you give me back my wife!"

Laughter swirled around him, then a familiar voice spoke. "What makes you think that's a viable option?"

He expected a bit of negotiation, but not a flat-out refusal. "But...you've been going after Sally for weeks now."

"Weeks? You should learn to pay closer attention, old man."

Sally pulled free from his grip, then turned to meet his gaze. The smile on her face sent a chill through his blood. The voice had belonged to her.

"I've been going to Baymell since I could walk, Grandpa. You were too busy worrying about Grandma, or my bat shit crazy mom to notice me. It wasn't until you wanted to *use* me to get your precious wife back that you cared about anything I did."

She grabbed her grandfather by the front of his shirt, and pulled him through the portal. The ground shifted beneath his feet, his body weightless and spinning. He squeezed his eyes closed and held out his arms to brace for the eventual impact, but the sensation quickly faded as he felt solid ground beneath his feet. He slowly opened his eyes, and gaped at the landscape before him.

Dark, rolling hills spread left and right, dotted with the skeletal remains of blackened, leafless trees. What he supposed was their moon, or perhaps the sun, shone wan, blue light across the land, creating blurred shadows of everything in its path. He stared down at the cracked, cobblestone road. Dark blue and green weeds, spikey, thick, and glistening, pushed their way through the cracks, their thorns dripping with white, milky fluid.

A rough chittering sound caught his attention, and he looked at the nearest tree. Several mangy and scraggly animals, like emaciated squirrels, chased one another around its base. The smallest creature, clutching something tiny and round in its teeth, evaded the bigger animals until it stumbled over a protruding root. It dropped the object it had been carrying, then stared at the others as it backed away. The largest creature sniffed at the item. It snarled, then pounced on the tiny animal, tearing and shredding its body as the other beasties snapped up the fallen object and bounded away.

He swallowed hard, and grimaced. A low rumbling floated to his ears, and he turned to find its source. Pulled by a team of six horse-like animals, large well-muscled beasts the color of emeralds smudged with soot, a black and silver ornate carriage lumbered up the road toward him. His granddaughter, still gripping his shirt, pulled him out of its path. The carriage rolled to a stop directly in front of them. The driver, a squat, wart-covered man, hopped down, arched an eyebrow at the older man in Sally's grip, then released a set of small steps from underneath the carriage.

When the man reached up and pulled open the small door in the side of the hansom, Sally knelt, then pulled her grandfather to the ground with a sudden force that cracked his knee against the edge of a stone. He toppled to his side, grasping his injured joint. He felt a sticky warmth through his slacks, and realized he was bleeding.

"Grandpa, kneel properly," Sally grunted at him.

When he didn't right himself fast enough, she grabbed his arm, and yanked him up. Once he was positioned to her satisfaction, Sally gripped the back of his neck, and whispered into his ear.

"Show the proper respect."

She pushed him forward at the waist until his forehead pressed against the road. He heard a husky voice come from above him.

"That's not necessary, child. Release him."

She clutched her hand to her chest, and bowed her head. "Forgive me, my Queen. But he–"

"I know all about his plans."

"Of course, I'm sorry."

Grandpa risked a glance up at the carriage. A beautiful, statuesque woman towered over him. He unfolded his body, and stared straight up at her, his fear momentarily forgotten. Even though she was incredibly tall and thin, her skin the color of a storm-filled sky, the likeness was unmistakable.

"Margerie? Is that you?"

The woman chuckled, covering her mouth with long, slim fingers. "Naturally you would mistake me for your wife. The people have always said she was almost an exact copy of me at her birth."

He frowned, not quite understanding. She laughed again while Sally snickered.

"You know her as Margerie, but here she is Morigayne, my daughter."

The air suddenly felt thick, and he couldn't breathe. He pulled the collar of his shirt away from his neck, but his heart thumped in a panicked rhythm, and small black dots swam in his vision. Sally stared at him, her mouth curled up in a cruel smile, but the elegant woman from the carriage stepped over to him, and placed a hand against his back.

"I know. It's a lot to take in. Just breathe slowly. Breathe..."

Her words soothed him, and he recovered quickly. He straightened to look at her again, and his mouth relaxed into a smile. She mirrored his expression.

"There now. Better?"

He nodded. "Much, thank you."

"Good. Guards!"

She straightened and stepped back as two burly hulks appeared on either side of him, and pulled him to his feet. His back cracked at the sudden shift, and he winced. Their vise grips soon had his hands tingling from lack of circulation. The Queen flicked her eyes to look at the far horizon.

"Take him to the castle, and secure him in the dungeon."

As the two brutes yanked him up and began to drag him away, the Queen stopped them. "Wait."

Grandpa felt a brief sense of relief until she flashed her glistening teeth in a savage smile. She approached him, then hooked a sharp-nailed finger under his chin.

"Take him to Folamh."

As the large creatures holding him sneered, they changed direction and headed west, toward a low range of dark, craggy hills. A sudden gust of wind blew across those knolls and swirled around him, carrying the foul stench of blood and rot. Grandpa craned his head to look back at Sally.

"Sally, help me! Don't let them do this."

His granddaughter simply stared at him, folding her arms across her chest. The Queen moved beside her, placing her long, thin arm around Sally's shoulders, and pulled her close. She looked upon him with pity as she shook her head.

"There's no one to help you here, Donald. Your

treachery alone has determined the end time of your life. But I would have sent you to The Empty One anyway, simply for the mere pleasure of knowing you would die in horrible, twisting agony. All of your kind should meet such a fate."

He continued to struggle against his captors, but they were too strong. They carried him away as easily as a parent might scoop up an infant from its bassinet. His screams were ignored as he was dragged to his doom.

The Queen and Sally stood watching him as he faded into the darkness, his thrashing form like the helpless worm at the end of a large and terrible hook. Sally smirked when the Queen's low chuckle floated on the evening wind.

"Come, Siobhan. We must continue our plans. With Morigayne back home, and you by my side, Baymell will soon be hidden no more."

Sally/Siobhan wrapped her arms around her great-grandmother's waist, and lay her head against the woman's breast.

"We have the cellar door for now, but soon we'll connect to more through my old neighborhood, and eventually across the country. And then–"

"The whole human world will be within our grasp."

Siobhan smiled up at the Queen. "And then?"

The Queen's grey skin shone in the blue light of Baymell's moon, her silver eyes flashing with power.

"Any then, my darling child, all worlds will be ours for the taking."

The entwined pair turned toward the carriage. The squat attendant jumped down from the driver's seat, and extended the steps once more. Opening the door, he offered a warty hand first to the Queen, and then to Siobhan, as each entered the conveyance. After securing the small door, the Queen called out through the open window.

"Return us slowly, Corgund. Let us enjoy the warm evening air. I'm afraid this mild weather will be our last before the ice season settles in."

"Of course, my Queen," he rasped.

Hopping back atop the carriage, the driver urged the bridled beasts into motion, heading toward the glistening, black spires of the castle.

ABOUT THE AUTHOR

Peggy Christie is an author of horror and dark fiction. Her work has appeared in dozens of websites, magazines, and anthologies, including *13 Little Hells*, *Necrotic Tissue*, and *Fearotica: An Anthology of Erotic Horror*. You can find her first short story collection, *Hell Hath No Fury*, from Dragons Roost Press, and her vampire novel, *The Vessel*, from Source Point Press. Peggy is one of the founding members of the Great Lakes Association of Horror Writers, as well as a contributing writer for the websites of Cinema Head Cheese and Slack Jaw Punks. Check out her webpage at themonkeyisin.com for more information on her other publications, and appearances.

Peggy loves Korean dramas, survival horror video games, and chocolate (not necessarily in that order) and lives in Michigan with her husband and their dog, Dozer.

DRAGON'S ROOST PRESS

Dragon's Roost Press is the fever dream brainchild of dark speculative fiction author Michael Cieslak. Since 2014, their goal has been to find the best speculative fiction authors and share their work with the public. For more information about Dragon's Roost Press and their publications, please visit:

http://thedragonsroost.net/styled-3/index.html.

ALSO AVAILABLE FROM
DRAGON'S ROOST PRESS

Ever wonder how you might handle a sabbatical from work? Think the bible told you everything there is to know about the Devil? What if the noises coming from under your child's bed weren't just in his imagination? Crack open Hell Hath No Fury, a collection of 21 tales of horror and dark fiction, to learn the answers to these questions. Discover stories of psychotic delusions, ghosts, a murder victim's revenge, and a family brought closer together through torture. All of this and more awaits inside this collection of stories from horror master Peggy Christie.

Cryptozoology -- "the study of hidden animals"
The search for and study of animals whose existence or survival is disputed or unsubstantiated

Menagerie: a strange or diverse collection of people or things.

Welcome to the Hidden Menagerie -- two collections of short fiction involving various cryptozoological creatures. In the first volume you will meet the beasts of the land. Inside these pages you will be introduced to new visions of some creatures you are familiar with like the Abominable Snowman and the Wendigo. In the second, the beasts of the air, sea, and animate vegetation — the Kraken, Mermaids, and Lake Monsters. Both volumes contain creatures long thought extinct which live on to this day, and others you may have never heard of. creatures long thought extinct which live on to this day, and others you may have never heard of.

Combine the mind splintering horror of the Cthulhu Mythos and the heart shattering portion of that most terrible of emotions - love - and what do you have? You have Eldritch Embraces: Putting the Love Back in Lovecraft. This collection of short stories from some of the best working in the fields of horror and dark speculative fiction blends romance and Lovecraft in a way which will may make you sigh, smile, weep, or leave you the hollow shell of your former self.

Robotic Animals, Televisions Which Reveal Alternate Universes, Inanimate Objects Brought to Life, People Struggling to Survive in Apocalyptic Wastelands, Sentient Cutlery, and much, much more.

Desolation: 21 Tales for Tails is a collection of dark speculative fiction whose stories all focus on themes of loneliness, isolation, and abandonment. Enter into strange worlds envisioned by some of the most inventive authors writing today. A portion of the proceeds of each sale of Desolation: 21 Tales for Tails benefits the Last Day Dog Rescue Organization.

In post-World War III, small town Michigan, a self-proclaimed, violent, and insane High Priestess has taken control, reducing the remaining men to nothing more than slaves and playthings. Jericho, the reluctant leader of the Resistance, must fight her own family to preserve the freedom and equality of all in her care - male and female alike. She's torn between love and duty, and with traitors around every corner, she has no idea who to trust anymore.

The battle is over, but the war has just begun. Jericho returns to the Obsidian camp, only to learn that her sister Candace destroyed it as part of a plot to dismantle the resistance movement that brought down their mother, the High Priestess. The rest of the resistance blames Jericho for the deaths of their friends, but that's the least of her worries. Not only does Jericho now have to right the wrongs her sister has done, she must contend with a few guests to the camp who bring secrets that will change her life forever. Either she'll redeem herself in the eyes of her comrades, or she'll die trying.

The best man on the pirate ship is a girl named Alex.

Alexandra "Alex" Gardner is the reluctant cabin boy on The Bloody Maiden, a ruthless pirate ship run by the charmingly evil Captain Montgomery. The crew is convinced she's a boy, and she hopes it stays that way until she has the chance to avenge the deaths of her mother and brother at the hands of the crew. All goes well until the ship takes a handsome captive. Could her feelings for him ruin her charade?

Sebastian Whitley is a young man in love. He sails on his father's ship, trying to find the beautiful girl he's lost. When he's captured by The Bloody Maiden, the annoying cabin boy saves his life – and makes it more difficult at the same time. His savior is actually a girl, and if Sebastian doesn't keep quiet, it could mean both their deaths. Together, they have to thwart a mutiny, get revenge, and get off the ship before Alex's secret is revealed. If not, it's the plank for both of them.

Do you enjoy creepy stories about people who don't quite fit in? Dead Girls Don't Love is a collection of poignant tales for the outsider in all of us.

For a domestic violence victim, there is no life after death--but could there be revenge?

Can a woman returning to her life after 40 years with the fae remember how to be human?

When two Buddhist monks travel to China to spread the dharma, will they survive the unspeakable horror they find instead?

What really happened when the Big Bad Wolf ate the lonely grandmother living in the woods?

Will the love between two zombified women help them break the spell that binds them in eternal servitude?

And, perhaps most importantly, can an Elder God find true love?

These and many more fascinating questions will be answered on the pages within, if you dare to read them. But be warned: the strange and horrifying realities contained in

Dead Girls Don't Love may haunt you long after you close the back cover.

Not long ago, Zuzanna Uritski was a cleaner at the 1893 Chicago World's Fair, Archibald Campion was the Fair's most imaginative engineer, and Elspeth was a lifeless automaton. But now? Now they're demon hunters, pursuing an ancient evil that has traveled across universes to take residence in one of history's most famous serial killers. Travel to an alternate history where no one is safe from demon possession, automatons are self-aware, and the world's greatest hope lies with a clever engineer, a dauntless young woman, and a paladin from another world.

Wait! Seriously, hang on a minute before opening this book. In case the title, and lurid, disturbing image on the front haven't already made it shockingly clear, THIS BOOK IS NOT FOR CHILDREN. Or people with sensitive stomachs. Or taste.

Enter the twisted mind of horror author Ken MacGregor as he explores the boundaries of horror, eroticism, and yes, taste.

Made in the USA
Middletown, DE
29 August 2022